BEN Books Present

BOBBY NASH PRESENTS

SNOW SHORTS!

COLLECTED VOLUMES

1

BOBBY NASH · GARY PHILLIPS · NICOLE GIVENS KURTZ

First BEN Books Ebook Edition 2021

WWW.BEN-BOOKS.COM

SNOW SHORTS COLLECTED EDITION #1
SNOW FLIES by Bobby Nash
THIEVES' ALLEY by Gary Phillips
A STRANGER CALLS by Nicole Givens Kurtz

© 2021 Bobby Nash
All Rights Reserved.
First BEN Books Printing.

Book Production and design by Bobby Nash.
Edited by Ben Ash Jr.& Michael Gordon
Cover Art/Design: Jeffrey Hayes

ISBN: 9798536941485

Published by BEN Books
PO Box 626, Bethlehem, GA 30620
www.BEN-Books.com

And so it begins…

Dedicated to the memory of our friend, Derrick Ferguson.

Derrick was more than a writer and creator, he was a supporter, a cheerleader, and a dear friend. Derrick was the soul of this thing we call New Pulp. As he liked to say, Derrick was the King of the Jungle, always happy to help.

He will be greatly missed.

BEN BOOKS PRESENTS…

Katelyn Snyder was running late.

First off, she forgot to set the alarm clock, or did she sleep through it? She wasn't sure which, though neither was a good thing. Of the two of them, Randy, her husband, was the morning riser. He was the one who got the kids up, washed, fed, and dressed before she even thought about opening her eyes. Her husband was a godsend, especially in the mornings.

So, naturally, his job thought it would be a grand idea to send him out if town for a week during the first week of the school year to a tech conference in Las Vegas.

Not going wasn't really an option for him, and she did not want to begrudge him his career, but she told him not to worry and that she could handle it. She reassured him several times that she was not angry and the trip was no big deal. Both were lies. It was a big deal. Katelyn felt abandoned and despite her promises to the contrary, she was pissed off nonetheless. It was irrational. She knew this, but that didn't stop the anger from bubbling to the surface.

The kids were no help either.

Karen, her thirteen-going-on-thirty daughter, wasn't speaking to her this week so no help was expected from that quarter. Good thing as none seemed to forthcoming no matter how much she asked. Patterson, her adorable little man, was a handful. She found the three-year-old's antics cute when Randy was dealing with them, but not so today.

By the time she dropped them at the high school and day care, respectively, Katelyn was roughly twenty minutes behind schedule and on her way to being late for work. Factor in Georgia rush hour traffic and she might as well have been two hours late. Jenkins is going to be pissed, she mused, not looking forward to listening to her much younger boss' tirade if she missed the morning meeting.

All of these issues played in her mind in a jumble, all of her frustrations tumbling around in the clothes dryers that was her brain. She worked out math equations in her head to determine if there would be enough time to stop by the coffee shop for her morning Grande, Iced, Sugar-Free, Vanilla Latte With Soy Milk and Danish or if she would have skip it and drink the swill they made in the office breakroom.

So focused on her own thoughts was she that she didn't hear the whole of the jumbo jet's engines until they were right on top of her.

Literally.

The plane screamed overhead, coming in low of the highway. Katelyn had no way to know that the pilot had called in an emergency landing and was going to set the plane down wherever he could.

The repair van in front of her hit the brakes hard, it's tires smoking rubber as it went into a skid.

Unable to stop in time, Katelyn slammed her SUV into the van's exposed side. The airbag erupted from the steering wheel into her face, shoving the glasses she wore into her face. She tasted blood from a nosebleed but was otherwise uninjured.

A tiny new Prius likewise crumpled her back bumper, the driver unable to stop in time or swerve out of the lane into the median. By the time it was over, the pile up included fourteen vehicles and one very large airplane. Thankfully, no one was seriously injured in the incident, but insurance investigators would be busy for a couple of weeks working out the logistics.

The airliner touched down in the asphalt that made up Georgia Highway 316, tired smoking on impact. Ironically, small airfield was less than a mile ahead, though, like the highway, it was not built to accommodate a plane as large as the 747.

In the days and weeks after the incident, many news stories would be reported on the incident that led to the emergency landing, most news outlets referring to it as *Crisis on Flight 248*. A group of individuals, their identities not yet revealed to the public, attempted to hijack Flight 248 en route from New York to Atlanta.

Even Katelyn Snyder had been interviewed by the local news on the scene as EMTs cleaned her up and made sure the airbag had not broken her nose. She had DVR'ed the report to show her husband when he returned from his trip. This would show him, she thought. This incident would keep him in town with her and the kids.

Reports varied, but the leading theory shared with the public by the Department of Homeland Security is that this group planned to crash the plane into the airport. Not only would this result in an untold number of casualties but would ground operations   at   Atlanta's   Hartsfield-Jackson

International Airport for weeks, maybe longer. By shutting down an international hub like Atlanta, the hijackers would have temporarily crippled numerous international flights.

The news stories also told the tale of former Air Force pilot, Calvin Hodge, who had been a passenger on the ill-fated flight. After the pilot was killed, Hodge and the in-flight air marshal launched an attack that took out the hijackers and, after finding the pilot dead and the co-pilot injured, the former Air Force pilot took control of the plane and performed an emergency landing, saving hundreds of passengers and preventing tragedy.

Overnight, Calvin Hodge became a media darling. Reporters dogged his every move, each one wanting just one word or a comment on what happened. The barrage was relentless. He was trotted onto CNN, MSNBC, and FOX News, hailed an American hero of the highest order. The Air Force even offered to give him an award and a substantial cash bonus if they could use him in their next recruitment initiative.

It was too much, too fast, and it threatened to overwhelm Hodge, so he retreated into old, familiar habits, bad habits, and got in over his head.

Suddenly, those same news outlets that praised his heroics switched gears and told the tale of a self-destructive man dealing with alcohol abuse issues, anger issues, and more. Public opinion swayed him from hero to villain within days of the landing. Frustrated, Hodge eventually stopped answering his phone, then he changed the number, cancelled all of social media accounts, and stopped answering his door. It helped for a time, but they were relentless and kept coming.

He called on an old friend to help him, offered a suggestion on how to help him, but his request had not been met with the excitement he had expected.

Eventually, the constant media attention got the best of him. On what appeared to be an average Tuesday, Calvin Hodge cut ties with everyone he knew, closed out his checking and savings accounts, sold his car, walked out on his apartment lease, and ran.

Once he was out of Atlanta, he fell off the radar.

Abraham Snow hated to fly.

This wasn't always the case. There was a time when he loved air travel. During his undercover days, using the carefully prepared alias James Shepperd, Snow crisscrossed the globe on private jets, drinking champagne in soft leather seats while beautiful women kept his glass refilled. Once, he even found himself inducted into the infamous mile-high club on one of those rare occasions when he and Daniela Cordoza had Miguel Ortega's private jet all to themselves. It was fun, but terrifying. With every bump of turbulence, he was convinced he was going to die.

Ortega was her boss, and the object of Snow's undercover operation. Back then, Snow worked for Mother, an unofficial branch of the United States' war on terror. Snow had been working undercover gigs for Mother for almost ten years before he had to give it up.

More precisely, when his cover was blown, and Miguel Ortega shot him and left him for dead on a South American airstrip. It was not the ideal method of retiring, but that was the end result of a bullet missing his heart by only half an inch.

Lying there on that blistering hot tarmac, Snow vaguely recalled an out of body sensation before crashing back to Earth where his bleeding form waited. When his people found him, Snow was strapped to a gurney and flown to the nearest medical facility. He couldn't say with any certainty that the out of body experience really happened or if it was a fever-induced hallucination, but that moment coupled with lying in the evac helicopter was when his nervousness about heights, most notably flying, began.

Since retiring from active operations, Mother allowed Snow to return to civilian life with his full benefits, pension, back pay, and an honorable discharge from the U.S. Army, which is where Mother had plucked him all those years earlier. While working under cover, the Army provided a cover for him in case anyone came looking for Abraham Snow. On paper, he had been serving in the Army since he enrolled at eighteen and was honorably discharged at thirty.

He was no good for undercover work these days, thanks to a blown cover and a bullet fragment lodged a half inch from his heart, but Snow remained a skilled operative and decent investigator. Mother agreed to his retirement with the proviso that, if he was needed, and Mother called, he damn well better answer the call.

He understood.

That's why, when General Pinkwell called and asked for a favor, Snow agreed on the spot. The General was an old family friend, working with both Snow and his grandfather, Archer Snow, who Abraham was surprised, though not really with his history, that his grandfather had also worked for Mother.

The general was worried about Calvin Hodge. Hodge did not work for Mother the same way the general did or Snow had, but he had helped out during one of Snow's undercover operations. The Air Force had loaned out Hodge to play a smuggler who Snow's alias, James Shepperd worked with on a previous gig. Snow and Hodge had not met prior to the operation, but at that time, Snow had been under a long time. It was nice to have someone he could talk to when it was just the two of them on a flight without fear of blowing his cover.

He and Hodge had worked well together and their mission had been a success. Mother's forces were able to track a weapons shipment back to its source and close off a supply line that fed weaponry to terrorists.

Snow owed Hodge one.

He suspected the general knew that, which is why he asked Snow for help instead of sending in one of Mother's active operatives. The general explained Hodge's with the media and Snow admitted that he had been as curious what was going on as anyone else. Hodge had approached the general with a mission. Because of the news stories reporting the hero pilot's gambling problems, he had been approached by some, well, he described them as *less than scrupulous men*, had paid him a visit with an offer to help wipe out his debts. That offer included Hodge smuggling for them.

Reluctantly, the general agreed to back Hodge's plan, on the understanding that he would keep in touch and not do anything reckless without the old man's approval. That did not happen and, after the pilot fell off the grid, Pinkwell got worried. Hodge didn't know any Top Secret details about Mother, only that General Pinkwell worked classified off the books missions, so he wasn't necessarily a security risk, but he was a good man and the general genuinely wanted to help him.

So did Snow.

He had a good idea where to start his search.

The plane rattled as it descended toward the runway, cracks and pops accompanying each bump as though the plane wanted to tear itself apart. The general's idea of transport was not a private jet or even first class on a jetliner. No, being a four-star, General Pinkwell simply had the next available transport placed on hold until Snow reached the airfield.

In this case, transport was a Douglas C-47 delivering cargo that had delivered a shipment of supplies a National Guard post just outside of Snow's hometown, Sommersville, Georgia.

He had just enough time to throw a few clothes in a duffle, grab his gear, and go. Not knowing how long he would be gone, Snow had his buddy, Big John give him a lift to the local airport. Thankfully, the plane was only held up twenty minutes. If they had been flying out of Atlanta, it could have been a couple of hours or more on the road before they arrived.

The plane was in the sky minutes after he checked in and stowed his gear.

Their destination: Fort Campbell, Kentucky.

General Pinkwell had someone waiting for Snow as soon as he stepped off the plane.

"Mr. Snow, welcome to Fort Campbell," the young lieutenant said as she offered a hand. "Lieutenant Danforth. General Pinkwell has assigned me to be your liaison while you're with us."

Snow shook it.

"A pleasure, Lieutenant Danforth. I believe you have some stuff for me."

"If you'll follow me, sir," she said and spun on her heel and headed toward a car that was idling nearby, waiting for them. She held the rear passenger door open for him and he stepped inside, giving her a nod. Once inside, Snow felt the cool, welcoming blast of air conditioning.

Snow signed the papers that gave him possession of an unmarked car to use along with a small apartment off base that was used as a safe house part of the time or an off the books place to crash for anyone who needed it.

He stopped by the apartment long enough to shower, freshen up a bit, and check in with the general. The old man was none-to-pleased by

Snow's non-answer when he asked is Snow knew where Hodges was holed up. All he would tell the general was that he had an idea he was following, nothing concrete.

The apartment was a small place with only minimal furnishings. It was spartan and no-nonsense, everything he expected a safe house to be. The apartment was only a rest stop, however. Snow still had a long drive ahead of him.

Snow pointed his car north west and made the one-hundred-mile sojourn to Metropolis, Illinois. The town was small, kept in business by the tourist trade as millions came through each year to visit the home of Superman, stop by the museum, and get their photo taken with the fifteen-foot-tall statue of the Man of Steel.

The other big attraction was the casino.

Floating on top of the Ohio River, the casino was landlocked, but still technically a floating gaming house. The only way to operate a casino in the area was to be on an Indian Reservation or on the water.

Snow remembered that Hodge liked to gamble. He also recalled that the man wasn't a very good gambler, which is what got him into trouble in the first place. The pilot had told a few stories about time spent at the Metropolis casino. To Hodge it was a familiar place, somewhere he felt safe.

For Snow, it seemed like as good a place as any to start his search.

He checked into the hotel attached to the casino and asked if Calvin Hodge had already checked in. The woman working the check in desk would not divulge the information, despite his story about them being old friends with plans to meet up this weekend for a few fun days of gambling.

Thankfully, Hodge preferred this casino. Had he gone to Vegas, finding him would be a lot more difficult based on the size and number of people who frequented the Vegas Strip. Metropolis was busy, but manageable. There were also a lot fewer Elvis impersonators, which he found comforting. Something about grown men cosplaying a long dead rock star gave him the creeps.

Snow had only been on the floor twenty minutes when he spotted Hodge shooting Craps.

The boy was on a hot streak and the crowd cheered as he rolled another good number. Snow walked up next to him and clapped a hand on his friend's shoulder, startling him.

Hodge gave Snow a look and a smile, then turned his attention back to the game before he realized who it was who had spoken to him. He looked back at the wild-haired man with a big, dumb smile as he scooped up the dice the dealer pushed his way.

"Shep!" Hodge shouted and threw an arm around Snow's neck, the dice still clenched in his fist. "Holy, hell, son! What brings you here?"

Snow opened his mouth, but Hodge pushed on before he could speak.

"You're just in time to watch me break the bank!"

The pilot was acting drunk, slurring his words and swaying ever so slightly off balance, but when he hugged Snow, there wasn't more than a hint of alcohol on him, and that was on his shirt, not his breath. He was pretending to be drunk. Snow wondered why but held the question until they were alone. If Hodge was working a case, as Pinkwell intimated, the last thing Snow wanted to do was blow his plan by asking untoward questions in public.

Oblivious to Snow's concerns, Hodge pushed the large stack of chips in front of him onto the table. The stack fell over like a scene out of a Hollywood movie. "What say we let this ride?" he told the dealer, an older woman who seemed incapable of expression.

She nodded and the dealer on the stick called for last bets.

"What do you think? You feeling lucky, Shep?" Hodge said loudly, once again calling Snow by his old under cover alias.

"Ah, what the hell?" Snow said and tossed a fifty dollar-bill at the dealer, who scooped it up and pushed it into the cash slot and replaced the bill with a fifty-dollar chip before the better could change his mind. "Roll 'em!"

Hodge rattled the dice around in his fist, mumbling incoherently about mama needing a pair of something or other he couldn't quite make out.

He tossed the bones and everything came up roses.

"Eleven!"

"Yes!" Hodge pumped his fist.

"Winnah!" the dealer announced and Hodge howled like Wolfman Jack reincarnated to celebrate his victory. Then, he reached over and planted a big, sloppy kiss on the beautiful woman in the slinky dress standing next to him.

At first, she was startled and Snow assumed his friend was about to get slapped, but then Hodge flipped her a fifty dollar chip and her surprised expression was replaced by a big, toothy smile.

Several stacks of chips were slid in front of the shooter and Hodge looked down at it, then to the woman at his side, a sultry redhead wearing a low cut deep purple dress with no bra and dark panties that showed through the nearly translucent material. She was a looker and her outfit left little to the imagination. She clung to Snow's friend like a drowning woman held a life preserver. She was attracted to winners. If Hodge's luck kept up the way it was going, it was a good bet she would accompany him back to one of their hotel rooms.

"What do you think, darlin? Ride it again?" Hodge asked her.

"Giddyup," she added playfully. Gambling was easier with someone else's money. No risk.

"Let it ride," Hodge said before looking at Snow. "You in?"

"Sure," Snow said, dropping one of his chips onto the table, holding the one he won back.

"Pussy," Hodge said with a smile as he let the red head blow on the dice. He shook his fist then launched the dice across the table.

"Winnah!" the dealer shouted once again and slid a large stack of chips at Hodge.

Snow scooped up his two coins, flipping the one that won into the air and catching it in his other hand.

"What say you and me quit while we're ahead and go grab a drink, huh?"

"Just one more, buddy! Come on! I'm on a roll!"

Snow shook his head.

"Sorry, folks," Hodge told the crowd. "My buddy here is making me quit."

The crowd booed Snow, who shot his friend a dirty look.

Hodge laughed and shouted, "One more time! Let her ride!"

He threw the dice before his friend could object.

Snow could have predicted what came next with his eyes closed.

"Snake eyes!"

The table let out a collective "*Awwww...*" as Hodge's chips were taken away by the dealer's stick, his hot streak officially at an end.

Snow put a friendly arm around his slumped shoulders and led him away from the table as a new shooter stepped in to take his place. Instantly, the crowd started cheering on the new player, already forgetting Calvin Hodge's impressive run.

"I told you to quit while you were ahead," Snow said, holding up his two chips for Hodge to see.

"I guess that means you're buying the first couple rounds, buddy," Hodge said, still laughing as though he had not just blown three grand on a lousy roll of the dice.

"I assume you know you've got a shadow," Snow whispered as they walked toward the bar situated just off the gaming floor.

"Yeah. They've been eye-balling me since I got here."

"I'm guessing they're the reason you intentionally blew that game back there?" Snow asked.

"You noticed that, huh? Well, lucky for me, not everyone is as observant as you are, old buddy."

They stepped into the bar. It was a modest place decorated in casino chic. The walls were intentionally scuffed, giving it an aged look. One wall showed exposed red brick that had started to blacken over time. The floors were polished hardwood and lighting fixtures made out of antlers hung from the ceiling over the various tables and the bar. A buffet sat along the far wall opposite the bar. There was a long line at the buffet, mostly retirees getting in an early supper or the late-night gambling crew carbo loading before heading into the casino to try their luck.

A waitress looked their way when they entered. Snow held up two fingers and pointed toward an empty booth in the corner.

She nodded and they headed over.

A couple of minutes later, a bottle of beer sat in front of each of them. Hodge ordered a bourbon as well, one for each of them, despite Snow's objection.

"I take it these are the guys you told the general about," Snow said once they were alone. The booths around them were empty and Snow had chosen a seat where he could keep an eye on the entrance. This was the closest they were going to have to a private conversation inside the casino. He fished the wallet out of his pocket and removed the cash and his hotel key. The bills went into his shirt pocket and the wallet he pressed between the seat cushion and the wall where he could find it later. It wouldn't do for Hodge's shadows to find drivers license and credit cards with Abraham Snow on them instead of James Shepperd if they decided to risk him.

If Hodge noticed, he said nothing.

"Their boss, actually," Hodge finally said. "I still can't believe you're here, man. Last I heard, you had retired or something. I figured you'd be lounging on a tropical beach somewhere with a coconut shell drink on one hand and a bikini clad island girl in the other."

"Retired yes," Snow said, taking a pull off his bottle. "But I'm a long way from the beach, believe me."

"Well, hell, I appreciate you coming to back me up."

Snow leaned in closer.

"About that. The old man said you broke contact. He sent me to find you. For some reason, he thinks you've gone and gotten yourself in deep."

"Deep enough."

"What does that even mean, Cal?"

"Are you familiar with the Dixie Mafia?"

"Yeah. I've heard of them. Are these guys…?"

Hodge smiled. "Sorta. They're private contractors, but they make sure to kick back their required cut to stay ion good with the local chapter."

"What are they moving?" Snow asked.

"Nothing illegal," Hodge said.

Snow gave him an *I don't believe you* look.

"Okay. These guys buy up cigarettes in Kentucky, Missouri, places like that where the taxes on them are low. Then, they truck them up to Chicago and New York and sell them to small mom and pop grocery chains that can't afford to pay the higher taxes in those cities. Occasionally, they bring in some from out of the country for those clients that can afford it."

"Isn't that still called smuggling?" Snow asked. "If you were talking booze, it would be bootlegging."

"This ain't Smokey and the Bandit, pal."

"No. It's not," Snow said seriously. "This seems small time. What do they need from you?"

"The Illinois State Police have gotten wise to their operation and has been clamping down on trucks on the highway. They want me to fly their cargo."

"Cigarettes?"

"And their bag men. They use teenagers, runaways, I'm told, to make the sales calls and deliveries."

"Are they taking these runaway kids across state lines?"

"Yeah. I think so. Why?"

"Because that's kidnapping and that is a major crime."

"Oh."

"Why you? The Dixie Mafia doesn't have pilots of their own, they need to go to an outsider?"

"Pilots, yes, but we're not talking airport to airport. No, no. These guys are using farmland, cow pastures, even the river. They need someone who can park a bird on a dime every time."

"And after seeing your story on the news landing that big ol' plane on a highway, they're convinced that's you."

"Something like that."

"But why? I'm sure these guys checked you out. What makes them think you'd be willing to go along with this. You're high profile right now. Why risk it?"

"The general did some shuffling with my record. Turns out I was dishonorably discharged from the Air Force for disciplinary reasons and there were rumors I was part of a team looting war zones and smuggling the goods back home. And then there's my gambling problem…"

"So they're squeezing you over gambling debts?"

"Yeah. They bought my debt off of a bookie out of Chicago. They aren't real debts though. I mean, not really. I lost that money on purpose so they would approach me. All part of the plan."

"And the general is covering those tabs?" Snow asked.

Hodge's insincere smile made Snow wince.

"He didn't say no, but since I did it without his say so, the old man's a bit miffed. I'm sure he'll come through for me though."

"You better hope so," Snow said. "We've got company."

There were two of them.

One was tall, easily six foot. He was stocky, but not overweight. He looked like a guy who could handle himself in a fight. His orange-brown hair was long and looked greasy, at least the parts Snow could see sticking out from underneath the well-worn brown cowboy hat. The rest of the man's ensemble was right out of bad guy 101. Black jeans with a faded rock band t-shirt, Metallica as best Snow could see that the black leather jacket did not conceal. His light beard was patchy and ungroomed, and he chewed on a matchstick. Of the two of them, Snow assumed he was the brains of their particular operation.

The second man was the muscle. He wore jeans and a t-shirt as well, the shirt at least one, maybe two X's too small and tight around his large arms and stomach. He too wore a leather jacket, though not as nice as his partners. He was bald, shaved close so only stubble remained. His face was hidden behind a thick, full dark beard that started at his ears and flared out to the sides and covered his double chin.

"Gentlemen," the skinnier of the two said as he approached their table, removing his hat as polite company did when interrupting a private conversation.

"Hi, there," Snow said, staring at the man and sizing him up.

The wound in his chest from being shot was more or less healed, though a small piece of shrapnel remained lodged in some muscle tissue where it was hard to reach safely. While he could still handle himself, Snow hated to admit that he wasn't as indestructible as he once thought. His doctors had warned him repeatedly to take things slow and easy. With his injuries, a heart attack was not out of the realm of possibility.

Suffice to say, Snow hadn't listened to their advice as well as he should have since being discharged from the hospital.

"Howdy, Mr. Hodge," the tall man said. "We were looking for you inside. Did you forget our appointment?"

Hodge smiled. "Not at all. We've been right here waiting for you."

"We?"

"Where are my manners," Hodge said. He motioned toward Snow. "James Shepperd, allow me to introduce Mr. Sam Pike and his associate, Bear."

"Bear?" Snow mouthed.

Hodge raised an eyebrow.

"Have a seat," Hodge said, sliding in so Pike could sit next to him. Bear was a big guy. There was no way he would be able to slide into the booth next to Snow.

"Grab a chair," Snow told him, pointing to an empty one at a nearby table.

"He'll stand," Pike said, even though Bear had already started reaching for the chair. After hearing his partner's comment, he stopped, leaned against the wall and crossed his arms over his chest.

"Whatever works," Snow said.

"Who is this guy?" Pike asked Hodge.

"My partner."

"You never said nothing about no partner before."

"You never asked about my partner before," Hodge said.

It looked like Pike was ready to bolt.

"Do you think I do all of this by myself? I mean, I'm flattered that your employer thinks I'm that good, but we're a two-man operation. Sometimes, three if it's a big enough haul and I have to get my cousin involved."

Snow's eyes darted between the men. He was afraid Hodge was going to overplay it and scare off Pike. If that happened, then the deal would fall apart and he could call the general and tell him mission accomplished. Or, they could stay in and find out who was behind the smuggling ring.

"Look, it's simple," Snow said to Pike. "He flies the plane. I handle the inventory. Everything remains above board and everybody walks away happy. It's a simple business operation and Hodge and I have been working this way for years, so you take it as is or we shake hands and walk away. Frankly, I'm good either way."

Pike turned his head and looked at Hodge. "You good either way too?"

Hodge stared blankly for a moment, then smiled. "Absolutely."

"Your call," Snow said.

"I don't know you, man," Pike said.

"James Shepperd." Snow reached out to shake his hand. "A pleasure to meet you."

Pike looked at the hand as if it were a serpent ready to strike. A second ticked by, then another before he shook Snow's hand.

"Now you know me," Snow said.

"Just like you know me," Hodge added.

"You got some ID on ya?" Pike asked Snow.

Snow smiled. "Nope."

"What do you mean '*nope*'?"

"I don't carry ID when I'm on the job," Snow said, snorting derisively at the mere suggestion. "When I'm on the job, anonymity is my friend and yours."

Snow pointed a finger at him.

"Trust me, you want me to remain anonymous."

Pike looked from Snow to Hodge and back again, clearly working through his limited options. If this was his operation, then walking away might be an option, but Snow knew from the moment he introduced himself that Sam Pike, if that was even his real name, was not in charge of this operation. Unless his boss pulled the plug, Pike was on the hook.

"Well, what's it going to be?" Snow asked.

Pike pulled a slip of folded paper from his jacket pocket and handed it over to Hodge, but his eyes stayed focused on Snow.

"Be at this spot at five a.m. Make sure you've got a good atlas. GPS signal gets a little spotty out here along the river."

"We'll be there," Hodge said.

"See that you are," Pike said before sliding out of the booth. "I'll see you gents in the morning," he said and tucked his greasy hair back underneath the cowboy hat.

Snow offered a half-assed salute.

"Let's go," Pike said to his partner, who followed him out without a word.

"You trust these guys?" Snow asked Hodge once they were gone.

"Nope, but it's their boss who hired me. These guys are just local muscle."

Snow retrieved his wallet and stuck it inside his jacket pocket.

"Do you actually have a plane?"

"Of course," Hodge said, a look of hurt crossing his features. "They asked for a plane capable of making a water landing. I talked a buddy of mine to loan me his. It's covered."

"Can it be traced back to him?"

"No. As far as anyone knows, he sold it months ago."

Snow and Hodge grabbed their dinner to go.

They walked from the casino across the parking lot that overlooked the muddy Ohio River on their way to the hotel. Snow was fairly certain they weren't being followed, but he still took a few odd turns to get back to the hotel and up to his room.

The room looked just as he left it when he flipped on the lights.

"Man, I'm starving," Hodge said as he started unbagging the food and loudly dropping ice into glasses.

It was part of the plan they had discussed on the way over. Although there was no way for Pike and Bear to know that Hodge had a partner, much less his name or where he was staying, Snow took precautions and swept the room for bugs while he and Hodge carried on an innocuous back and forth about the food, old times, and their respective bad luck at the gaming tables.

"It's clear," Snow finally said and tossed the detector on the bed.

"That's a relief. Did you really expect to find anything?" Hodge asked. "They didn't know you were here so how could they bug your room?"

"I prefer not to leave anything to chance," Snow said, peeking out the curtains that overlooked the massive parking lot below. Headlights were steadily moving in and out of the lot as the casino business picked up.

Snow pulled the phone and called Lieutenant Karen Danforth's personal live at Fort Campbell.

She answered on the first ring.

"Let the old man know I've made contact with the prodigal son. We've got a meeting in the morning at oh five hundred."

"I will pass that along," Danforth said. "Is there anything else I can do for you, sir?"

"As a matter of fact," Snow said, smiling. "I do have one small favor to ask."

"Of course."

"Do you have any drones?"

As it was wont to do, 5 a.m. came way too early.

Snow was a night owl so getting up before the first cock-a-doodle-doo was not exactly his idea of fun. He rolled out of bed at 3:30 a.m. and checked the casino parking lot again, not surprised to see it was still rather full despite the early hour. He called Hodge's room to make sure he was awake before he stepped into the shower. Normally, Snow preferred long, hot showers. He would stand beneath the warm water and feel the tension in his shoulders melt away. That was at home. In the hotel, he stood taller than the shower head and the water never passed lukewarm so he was in and out fast and dressed in plenty of time to meet Hodge downstairs.

He checked his emails. Nothing new except a meme featuring a MacGyver-ism sent to him by his buddy, Mac. He replied with a laughing emoji and slipped the phone into his pocket. He checked and holstered his weapon and left a Do Not Disturb sign on the door before heading out.

Calvin Hodge was drinking a cup of coffee in the lobby when Snow arrived.

"Good morning," he said, smiling cheerfully, which made Snow want to strangle him.

"Is that any good?" he asked, pointing toward the coffee.

"Freshest it's likely to be all day," Hodge joked and pointed to the machine nearby.

Snow poured himself a cup and dropped a couple of sugar packets worth into the dark liquid.

"How'd you sleep?"

Snow gave him a *go to hell* look.

"Not a morning person, I take it?"

"You could say that," Snow said. "I'm usually going to bed right around now. Getting up this early should be considered a sin."

Hodge laughed.

"Weren't you in the Army, soldier?"

"Well, there's the Army and then there's the *Army*," Snow said. Even though Hodge knew that he had spent time undercover, he wasn't sure how much the man knew about *Mother*. He didn't think the general had told him everything about the organization and Snow was not ready to be the one to betray that classified data.

"Say no more," Hodge said. "You ready to go?"

"As ready as I'll ever be," Snow said and motioned for his friend to lead the way.

"Let's take your car," Snow said. "I suspect they already know what it looks like. Best not to spook them."

"Good idea. You think your friend, the lieutenant, was able to…" Hodge started.

Snow cut him off with a slice of his hand through the air.

"She knows her job," he said as he slid into the passenger seat. "Right now, all we can do is focus on ours."

Pike and Bear were waiting on them when they arrived.

Both men were standing near a beat up old 70's vintage Chevy van that had been an attractive shade of blue at one time, back before the rust and bondo camouflage was added. Pike was smoking a cigarette and sipping a steaming cup of gas station coffee. Bear simply stood there, arms folded across his massive chest. If not for the small puffs of steam around his nose, Snow would have sworn the man was a statue. Or dead.

Pike pulled a long drag off of his cigarette and tossed it away with a flick of his finger when he saw them pull up.

The location was basically an empty field, nothing special or out of the ordinary. The selling point was that the field sat along the edge of the Ohio River, but could not be seen from the main highway, which made it ideal for smugglers.

A floatplane was tied to a couple of trees along the river's edge, bobbing up and down with the river's motion. They kept it landlocked while two other men that Snow did not know loaded boxes into the plane for transport. These two were young, probably sixteen or seventeen. This fit with what Hodge had told him about the smuggler's M.O.

In addition to the floatplane and old van, a helicopter was also parked in the field, the pilot leaning against it, smoking a cigarette. It was a small helicopter that Snow recognized as a Bell, circa the early 1980's at best. It was fast and maneuverable, but too small to effectively smuggle the number of boxes Pike was blackmailing Hodge to deliver. He assumed this was a follow vehicle, until they were sure they could trust Hodge and Shepperd.

"Good morning," Snow said, faking a cheerful demeanor.

Pike did not return the greeting, preferring to grunt instead. "It's about time you got here," he said after Hodge and Snow had both exited the car.

Hodge looked at his watch and frowned.

"I'm reading ten till," he said.

"I thought you was military," Pike said. "You Army types are supposed to be punctual."

"Air Force," Hodge said. "And that was a long time ago."

"Then you should know if you're on time, you're late," Pike said.

"I guess it's good we're here ten minutes early the, huh?" Snow added, not bothering to hide the sarcasm dripping from each word.

Pike puffed up, ready for an altercation.

"That the plane?" Snow asked, ignoring Pike's alpha male reminder and chucking a thumb in the direction of the seaplane and the two teenagers loading the boxes into it.

"What do you think?"

"Easy, man," Snow said. "We're all on the same side here. It was just a question."

"Are we?" Pike demanded.

"Are we what?"

"On the same side?"

"Unless you've got something to share with the rest of us that we don't already know, yeah," Snow said. "Look, you hired me and my partner to move your merchandise so let us do our job so we can all get paid and move on with our lives. How's that sound?"

Pike's cheeks reddened. Snow wasn't sure why he seemed so willing to blow the operation over petty posturing, but the man's attitude made the hairs on his neck stand up.

"Or we can walk away right now, if that's what you want," Snow added. "Pay us for our time and we're out of here. I'm good either way. Just say the word."

Pike's jaw clenched and unclenched.

"That's the plane," he said after a moment of tense silence.

"Go take a look," Snow told Hodge.

The pilot nodded, then headed to the plane for his pre-flight check.

"All we need now is the location to deliver the package," Snow said.

Pike flipped his wrist and like a magician's card trick, a small piece of folded yellow notebook paper appeared in his hand.

He handed the paper over to Snow. It contained coordinates.

"Someone will be there to meet you and take possession on your cargo," Pike said. "Then, you fly straight back here. At that point, our business will be concluded, and you'll be paid."

"Sounds good to me," Snow said.

Once Hodge gave the plane a thumbs up, Snow climbed on board and took the copilot seat as Hodge turned over the ignition. He glanced in the back at the boxes containing what he assumed were cigarettes, exactly as planned. The surprise was that the two teenagers were also sitting in the back, surrounded by boxes.

"You didn't say anything about passengers," he told Pike. "Especially not kids. Smuggling is one thing. Kidnapping is another."

"Lucky for you, you're not crossing any state lines."

"That's a fine hair to split," Hodge said, clearly unhappy with this new turn of events.

"What does it matter?" Pike asked. "Cargo's cargo and they ain't going to complain."

"I don't like surprises," Snow told him.

"And I don't completely trust you, Mr. Shepperd," Pike said. "They go or you all stay and we find ourselves another pilot."

Snow looked from Pike to the teenage boys to Hodge, and back again.

Hodge shrugged.

Snow repeated the pilot's gesture.

"I hope they don't get airsick," Snow said.

Pike smiled and Snow understood why he did not do so more often. Pike's teeth, they few that remained, were a rotten mess. He closed the door and slapped a hand against it twice.

Nearby, Bear untied the plane from the tree, allowing it to float free on the riverbank.

Snow threw Pike a salute as Hodge nudged the plane forward, pushing against the current. Seconds later, they were bouncing across the water, picking up speed until the plane's pontoons lifted free of the water and they were skyward.

"Nice takeoff," Snow told the pilot.

"That was the easy part," Hodge said.

Snow turned to look at their two passengers. They sat still, emotionless, and resigned to their lot in life.

"You aren't kidding," Snow muttered.

The flight was smooth sailing.

As suspected, the helicopter shadowed them for part of the trip before veering off and heading back in the direction it had come. It was the smart play. The last thing they needed to do was have a helicopter following the plane into Chicago. That might draw some unwanted attention. With them smuggling contraband, drawing attention to themselves was a bad idea.

"I guess that means they trust us," Hodge said once their shadow was no longer on their tale.

"Never assume that," Snow said.

Even the landing, which Snow was dreading, was nowhere near as bad as he had anticipated. Cameron Hodge truly was one hell of a pilot. The last time he had traveled with the pilot was in a large cargo plane and they were dodging a much smaller, but more heavily armed gunship over a mountain range. The smaller plane had all sorts of advantages over the flying brick they were in and it all came down to who was the better pilot.

Hodge flew literal circles around the other pilot, eventually crashing the smaller plane into a canyon wall and allowing Snow to complete his mission.

Of course, a few changes had happened since those days. Most notably, Snow had taken two bullets to the chest, and along with them, a fit of anxiety when it came to flying. Not that he planned to share that piece of information with Calvin Hodge.

Once they reached the coordinates, Hodge brought the plane in low until they were all but skimming the river's surface. Any pilot could fly the plane, but this landing, this was why they had recruited Calvin Hodge. The landing area was small and narrow, much like a road, Snow noted. There was absolutely zero margin for error. The pilot had to be good enough to thread the needle and land safely.

Thankfully, Hodge was that good. He brought the plane in for a perfect landing and coasted to the makeshift dock where Pike's compatriots were waiting for them.

Once the plane was tied off, Snow and Hodge exited the plane and met with the men in charge on this end of the supply chain. The two teenage boys quietly got to work unloading their cargo. Two other young men took the boxes from the dock to the waiting box truck where they were loaded. It was an efficient operation.

"Any problems?" the man watching them work asked. Like Pike, this guy was cocky and a bit overbearing. Definitely the man in charge on this end of the pipeline.

"Not on our end," Snow said.

"Good," the smuggler said. "On your return trip, we have a couple of boxes and passengers for you to take back with you."

"That wasn't part of our original bargain," Snow said.

"What difference does it make? You still have to fly the plane back. What's a couple more packages?"

"Well, for starters, that's extra weight," Hodge said. "We plan fuel consumption based on weight and distance. For seconds, it's added risk. We expect to be compensated for that risk."

"Are you saying you cannot accommodate our request?" the man in charge growled.

"No. That's not what I'm saying at all," Hodge said, not backing down.

"We just like to know these things up front is all," Snow interjected. "If we know what we're moving, we can plan accordingly and avoid any missteps. None of us here wants us running out of gas halfway there and having to ditch in the river, do we? I know I don't."

"Nor do I," Hodge said.

"Very well," the smuggler said. "Talk to Pike. Work out your bonus with him."

"I think we can do that," Snow said. "How long do you need to load your cargo?"

Hodge was not happy.

Once they were loaded and ready to go, Snow took his place in the co-pilot seat. There were fewer boxes this time around, but they were different sizes and shapes than those containing the contraband cigarettes they had delivered. Snow had hidden a tracker on the boxes as they were being unloaded. He hoped that would be enough for General Pinkwell to call in the Illinois State Police to stop the smugglers on this end of the pipeline.

If all went well, they would already be on the move against Pike and his crew at the other end. That was the good news. What the pilot was having a hard time accepting was seeing teenagers ferried back and forth this morning. The smugglers treated the cases of illicit cigarettes with better care than they treated these kids and it made Hodge's blood boil. It was all he could do not to imagine his little sister ending up in a similar position.

On board for the return trip were three young women. The oldest of them couldn't have been more than eighteen, but all of them looked worn down, emaciated from lack of proper nourishment. At least two of them had noticeable track marks on their arms indicating continuous drug use. Snow hated to think what else these girls had been forced into by Pike and his people.

"Are you ladies okay?" he asked, taking a chance that they weren't completely loyal to the people keeping them as virtual slaves.

None of them said a word, but the youngest gave a slight shake of her head.

"Look, moving smokes from one place to the other is one thing," Hodge added. "But you ladies have a choice in all of this. If you'd rather go anywhere else besides back to Pike, now's your chance to speak up."

Ever so slowly, the young ladies gave silent nods.

"All right then," Snow said. "Let me make a phone call. I'll have some friends meet us."

Snow gave Hodge a nod as he pulled the sat phone free from his jacket pocket and dialed. Lieutenant Danforth answered on the second ring.

"Everything in place?" Snow asked, dispensing with the pleasantries neither of them had time for anyway.

"Yes. The state police are moving to intercept the men in Chicago. We also found the warehouse your man, Pike is using as his base of operations. I have a team of state police and FBI agents waiting on our signal to move in on the warehouse. I did as you asked and gave your friend a call. Agent McClellan mobilized the local Bureau and got us some extra bodies quick. He'll have a team ready to move in on the landing zone on your signal."

"Copy that," Snow said into the phone. "We are en route and currently…"

He looked to Hodge, who mouthed the words, "*ten minutes.*"

"Ten minutes out," Snow continued.

Those ten minutes passed quickly.

"There's the LZ," Hodge said, pointing at the makeshift dock ahead.

On the bank sat the familiar vehicles they had seen before their early morning flight. That meant Pike and his people were waiting on them.

"And there's our welcoming committee," Snow said.

"I don't see your friends," Hodge said.

"Don't worry. They'll be here."

"They better be or we're toast."

"Why's that?" Snow asked, turning to follow the pilot's gaze.

"Because we've got company," Hodge said.

"Is that?"

"Yep. That's the helicopter that shadowed us earlier. Notice anything peculiar about it?"

"You mean other than it being armed to the teeth?" Snow said as he dialed the phone again. "Come on, Mac."

Hodge touched his headset as landing instructions were relayed to him from the ground. They were ordering him to land on the water. The floatplane was small, but it required a minimum of three thousand six hundred feet to land. He would have to take it down soon or their friends in the helicopter would assume there was a problem. Something told him that they were not the kind to ask questions before shooting.

"Copy that," he replied, shrugging at Snow's intense glare.

"We gotta land," Hodge said.

Snow held up a finger as he dialed again.

"Where are you, Mac?" he said as soon as his friend answered the phone. "We're boned up here. I'd rather not have to land right now."

"We're moving in now," Mac said.

"Careful," Snow said. "They have air support."

"Anything you can do about that?" Mac asked.

"I'll see what we can do."

He disconnected the call.

"Don't land," Snow told Hodge. FBI is moving in on Pike and his crew now. The only thing we have to worry about is…"

He was going to say *the helicopter*, but before he could put voice to the thought, the helicopter opened fire. Bullets smacked into the floatplane's thin skin, passing through the aluminum and plastic with ease.

Their passengers screamed and curled up tight, trying to make themselves as small a target as possible in the cramped space.

Moving on instinct, the pilot took the plane into a dive, heading straight toward the river below. He pulled up, skimming the floaters on the water and kicking up spray in their wake. The maneuver was not an easy one, but Calvin Hodge was no ordinary pilot, which is presumably why Pike and his people tried to recruit him to begin with. Before he started flying commercial jets, Calvin Hodge had been a decorated combat pilot. To him, landing that jetliner on the highway a few weeks prior was easy.

Evading an attack helicopter would be kid's stuff for him, Snow assumed.

"You can outrun this guy, right?" Snow asked, hands braced to keep him in his seat.

"The chopper? Yeah."

He turned hard to port and bullets peppered the plane's underside.

"The bullets? No."

"What can I do?" Snow asked.

"You got a gun?"

"Yeah."

Hodge pointed his head toward the plane coming up on their starboard side.

"Shoot 'em!"

Snow slid open the tiny side window and pushed his weapon through it. Taking aim was going to be tough, but Hodge was doing his best to line up a shot.

Snow squeezed off three shots. He couldn't be sure if any of the hit the target, but it was obviously enough to make them reconsider their offensive posture because the helicopter veered off. At best, he had bought them a few extra seconds.

Those seconds were all Hodge needed to put distance between them and the attack copter. He took the plane lower, gradually this time instead of a hard dive. They were flying only inches above the water now, trees zooming past as brown and green blurs.

They passed the dock at full speed.

Through the window, Snow saw FBI vehicles and agents taking the smugglers into custody. He grinned. At least that part of the plan was going well.

Snow heard the next round of gunfire before he saw the impact of several bullets fired close together missing the plane by inches and splashing into the river.

Then a few hit the wing and the plane shuddered its disapproval.

"No choice now," Hodge said and eased the plane down until the floaters were in the water. "We're down!"

"This guy's not going to give us time to dock," Snow said as the helicopter arced around to fly in for another pass.

"Can you swim?" he asked their scared passengers.

Head nods were his only answer.

Snow pushed open the door and helped them out.

"Quickly! Quickly! Swim toward those guys," he said, indicating the FBI agents on the bank. "Go! Now!"

The three girls hit the water and started paddling.

Hodge unhooked his seatbelt and climbed into the back. While he was getting out of the plane, Snow used the floater and the wing strut for support. He ejected and replaced the magazine on his weapon and waited for the helicopter's next run.

"Help them get to shore," he told Hodge.

"I'm not leaving you, man. I can help."

"You are helping. You help them. I help you. Circle of life, man. Now, move it!"

Snow heard a splash and trusted that Hodge had actually did as he was told. Snow kept his eyes focused on the helicopter. His handgun probably wasn't going to win against the automatic weapons mounted on the copter, but if he could hold them off long enough to buy Hodge and the girls time enough to get to safety, it would be enough.

The helicopter flew closer.

Machine guns roared to life, smacking the water all around Snow and the plane and chewing up pieces of it as well. The floatplane started to sink.

Snow opened fire and emptied his clip.

The copter's front windshield spider-webbed under multiple strikes, but it stayed on course.

Snow ejected the magazine.

He looked away from the oncoming helicopter and slapped a new magazine in place, his last one.

Back in place, he steadied himself the best he could on the sinking brick that was once an airplane. He fired again and again until the clip was empty.

"Shit!" With no time to contemplate his next move, Snow dove into the icy cold river just as the sections of the floatplane still above water were engulfed in fire.

Snow surfaced and chanced a look. He saw the fire and the copter, still bearing down on him. There was no way he could swim faster than the helicopter could fly so Snow braced for the inevitable impact.

Instead, gunfire erupted from the bank this time. The FBI agents had taken up position and opened fire, hitting the helicopter broadside and making it veer sharply and out of control. The helicopter slammed into the river, rotor blades snapping on impact.

Snow dove beneath the waves.

Smoke rose from the wreckage as it sank.

Neither the pilot nor gunner surfaced.

Before being gunned down on a South American airstrip, Abraham Snow had been a strong swimmer, had been able to hold his breath for upwards of three minutes and forty seconds, and had the endurance to go the distance. The post-shooting Snow found himself getting winded a lot easier than before. His swims were shorter and the thought of holding his breath longer than a minute and a half hurt.

After he broke the surface, Snow paddled toward shore, fighting against the river's current.

By the time he reached the bank, Hodge and Mac were waiting on him and helped Snow out of the water. He rolled over onto his back, steam rising off of him as the warmer temperature met the freezing cold water dripping of him.

Snow wheezed a thank you to his two friends.

"Everyone okay?"

"Safe and secured," Mac said.

"Good. Good."

Mac offered a hand up, but Snow waved it away.

"I think I'll lay right here a while," he mumbled.

Snow closed his eyes and enjoyed the sun's warmth.

###

A week had passed since the debriefing.

At General Pinkwell's insistence, Mac and the FBI received all of the credit for busting Pike and his smuggling crew, effectively shutting down both ends of the smuggling pipeline. The investigation was still ongoing as they tried to round up all of Pike's known associates and find and free the kids they had coopted into service. The first step in that plan was finding shelter for the three young ladies they had brought back from Chicago. DFACS would place them in foster care until their families could be found. The General assigned an operative to work with them as the girls could be called as material witnesses when this case eventually went to trial.

Calvin Hodge's inclusion in the operation was made public, though parts of it read like good fiction, and his hero status returned, as did his job flying jumbo jets back and forth from one end of the country to the other. According to the official report, Hodge had been working undercover for the FBI during the entire incident, including the bar fight. Snow had little doubt that Mother, through General Pinkwell, would keep Hodge on their speed dial in case they required his services again.

Snow's involvement was buried deep, which suited him just fine. He had spent too many years avoiding the spotlight and had no desire to seek it out now. He liked his anonymity, even if the bad guys never heard his real name. He was just happy that he had been able to recover his ID from the casino's bar.

The General sent along a token of his regard for helping out, a twenty-year old bottle of Snow's favorite scotch, which Abraham and his grandfather, Archer, shared on the balcony overlooking the lake after a fabulous steak dinner one evening.

Snow couldn't think of a better way to end the day.

The End.

BEN BOOKS PRESENTS...

Dr. Ri Jang Chol's finger hovered over the keyboard. Once he sent the virus into the mainframe it was only a matter of time before internal security's cyber division identified the source. Or at least they would arrest him along with the four others of the top echelon of Science Unit TZ-9. In all good consciousness, he wasn't going to remain silent while his colleagues were threatened with beatings and torture. He'd admit it was him once they came for them. Dr. Ri was going to miss the extra food rations and being able to freely explore the internet for two hours every other week to see what scientific doings were happening in the outer world. But such creature comforts were little solace if he allowed himself to be seduced by them and let his accidental discovery fall into *his* hands, the terrible Dear Leader. Yet like any proud parent, he couldn't turn his back on his creation -- not fully anyway. He'd managed to smuggle out a scan of his complete typed notes, calculations and diagrams. An atheist, how foolish had he been in doing so, praying the protocols he'd set up would see to it his notes were retrieved by ethical scientists. Or was it simply hubris, wanting to make sure his one and only bore his name as some persons or entity built a working prototype and thereby alter the course of conflicts and exploration. As if they'd give a damn about his wishes as by that time, he'd be dead and disposed of in an unmarked grave.

A death's head grin on his face, he pressed the key.

###

Laid out in a bleak terrain among sand and scrubs of cacti rests Sweetbrook maximum security prison in the Sonoran desert. It's a modern federal facility touted as escape proof. The prison is a series of one and a few two-story interconnected buildings, command towers at strategic intervals and an open-air recreation yard on a concrete pad. Over this area several propeller-driven drones equipped with cameras and pacifying gas maintained constant surveillance. The prison was patrolled by guards outfitted with the latest in security gear including a device that emitted sound waves detecting non-metallic objects beneath clothing. The institution utilized a variety of other advance technological measures to ensure its population remained compliant including motion sensors, remote controlled keyless doors, lasers and vibration sensors scanning the perimeter and vehicles for as much as an unexplained heartbeat. Radio frequency ID wristbands were worn by each convict.

Separated a football field distance from the main prison complex was a low, flat-roofed building of considerable size. This was the fulfillment center where prisoners with good behavior records got to work packing online orders from everything to shampoo to tennis shoes. In this structure in a soundproof section was also a call center for a smart TV manufacturer also staffed by the inmates. The loading dock where the trucks were lined up patrolled around the clock by guards, each outfitted with the aforementioned array of sensors and detectors.

Inside the prison's sleek hallways, the guards were supplemented by robot counterparts. These were not alloyed human simulacrums with artificial arms and legs though they did have a head. The machines were roughly chest high tall, triangularly shaped white molded plastic and metal, two by three feet at its base. Mobility was provided by treads. Their heads were constructed with microphones and 3D cameras linked to software designed to detect abnormal prisoner behavior. Each robot accessed a database of the usual patterns of the prisoners it interfaced with daily. The robo toasters as inmates called them patrolled autonomously but could be manually controlled as well.

Each prisoner in Sweetbrook to maintain phone privileges had been told when first incarcerated here to go to a particular room and say into the phone there a set of pre-determined phrases they were given. Phrases like "I see a kite flying in the breeze when I walk down the street." This was done to establish voice print analysis of the individual that would be useful identifying them in future situations should visual confirmation be compromised. Several prisoners refused to participate in this electronic information gathering and therefore had no phone privileges.

One of those prisoners unwilling to be recorded, as surreptitious recording was also regularly conducted at the prison was Orrin "Orrie" Childress. He was in his mid-seventies and had been a career criminal since the days he boosted cars as a teenager and engines had carburetors. He was housed in one of the other low-slung buildings that was part of the Sweetwater complex. As opposed to the light gray color of the rest of the buildings, it was painted beige. This was only his second time being locked down. The first had been at twenty-five and had been a four-year stretch. After doing his time, Childress had a successful run on the outside for some forty odd years. Time enough to consider going straight and did for a while but old dogs and new tricks. Long enough as well to acquire and blow through more than one fortune. But now the aging prisoner designated A559-008 was unwillingly a patient in the beige building, the prison hospital.

Like the rest of the prison, the hospital, and it wasn't a glorified infirmary, was well-scrubbed and professionally maintained. Unlike the majority of prisoners in here who shared space with others convalescing or hanging on, Childress was isolated in his own room. After clearing the security check, including a retina scan to be filed away digitally, John Salmon walked along the main polished corridors of the hospital. A temporary ID badge was clipped to the pocket of his unbuttoned plaid shirt over his black T, his broad chest straining the material. Several white clad orderlies, buffed men and women, gave the 6'5" muscular man the side-eye. He arrived at the one nurses' station in the facility. Next to this was a room containing a bank of monitors displaying each room with two guards on duty in there.

"I'm here to see Orrie Childress," he said to the pleasant-faced nurse who looked up at him.

"Yes, Mr. Salmon," she replied, consulting her computer screen. "I'll buzz you in."

"Thank you."

Salmon stood before the correct metal door inset with a thick square of break resistant polyacrylic allowing a view inside. Though he'd been prepared psychologically for this moment, the image of the older man lying in there with a tube and wires connected to his failing body gave the big man pause. The electronic lock of the door buzzed and turning the cold metal knob, Salmon entered. The door hissed closed behind him. Less than three full strides took him to Childress' bedside in the compact room. Momentarily he stood there looking down at his old friend who was dozing. There was a small wistful grin on the dying man's face. An oxygen tube was clipped to his nose. His eyes fluttered open and he smiled.

"Big Bad John," he said, his voice surprisingly strong. He was a light-skinned black man with thinning sandy colored hair, straight and cut short on his head. His features weren't much of a giveaway to his race. When Childress was younger, he'd pass for white. Not for social mobility but in the service of pulling off a score. With his glasses on and in a conservative suit, he looked like a school board member as opposed to a master thief. But that was then. Now he'd lost weight and his face was drawn from battling emphysema.

"Orrie. Sure as hell hate to see you like this."

"You and me both, brother." He turned his head toward a flat screen television mounted toward the ceiling in a corner of the room. It was on, the volume notched low, tuned to a long-running soap opera called *Harmony Lane*. A lithe attractive black woman of a certain age was lambasting a younger white woman. He returned his attention to his visitor.

"I was dreaming me and Miz Raquel had run away to a floating castle in the clouds over Ireland."

Salmon knew among other matters he was referring to the older actor on the screen, Raquel Wardlow. She'd been the reigning diva on the show for more than two decades.

"What do you need me to do, Orrie?" It was only when he received the call requesting him to come that he knew Childress was dying let alone had been sent back to prison. Apparently, he'd been incarcerated since last month. It wasn't that he didn't have feelings for this man, he did. But Childress was a pro, not given to sentimentality. If he'd wanted Salmon to only know he was dying, he would have simply told him such when he'd accepted the collect call from the prison. And he wouldn't have asked him to visit.

Childress started to speak again, but a raspy cough escaped his throat. The hacking continued and he shook a finger at plastic cup with a straw in it on the rollaway table. Salmon reached over and fetched it for him. Childress took several deep gulps and handed it back.

"I've got some personal things, some old photos, specialty tools, stuff like that I want you to take to Roe and the kids. It's with the ex and you know how them two don't get along." Rowena Childress was his daughter from a previous wife. His grandkids were nine and five.

"I hear you, man, no problem." He'd been standing next to the bed, one of his large hands on the railing. At one point, Childress had tapped that hand affectionately. Now Salmon sat down.

"What about you, Orrie, must be something I can get for you."

"Ain't no wresslin' this thing out of me, John. I figured to outrun it, but hell, I ain't got but a handful of regrets. I played out the string the best I could. I suppose I shouldn't have been a hardhead and got out like you did."

He smiled. "But the life was your drug of choice."

"Wasn't it?" he winked at him and began coughing again. Salmon stood to lean across for the water. This time the jag subsided quickly but he accepted the offered cup. Salmon remained standing, angled toward the bed. Childress finished and the big man put the cup back and sat down again.

"How about you? Heard you had a sweet gig, head mechanic in like that comedian, car nut guy's TV garage."

"Jay Leno you mean."

"Yeah."

"Not exactly but close enough." Behind him the door opened and in stepped a mahogany hued nurse. She was trim and had the shoulders of a swimmer. She carried a plastic pitcher and refilled the water cup.

"Hey, gorgeous," Childress beamed.

"Just coming to check on you, Orrie." She set the pitcher on the rollaway table.

"Ain't she something?"

Chuckling, Salmon said, "Careful, Orrie, it's a new day."

"I don't pay him no mind."

He stood to get out of her way as she checked the machines hooked into him. She was attentive to the one administering the oxygen.

"Your breathing okay today, Orrie?"

" 'Bout as well as can be expected, Claudia."

She made a sound in her throat and turned a dial on the oxygen machine. She fine-tuned several other machines, jotting down readings on Childress' chart. Afterward she returned the clipboard to its place at the foot of the bed. Then with a nod to both, she used her key card to open the door and left.

"They figure I got less than another month." Childress said devoid of emotion.

"Damn."

Childress spread his hands wide. "You roll the dice…"

"…and hope it ain't snake eyes." Salmon finished, taking his seat again.

They talked some more and Salmon, rising from the chair, told him he'd do his best to check in on him again.

"Ah, I hate being seen like this. I can't tell you how much I appreciate you coming to see me, John." He splayed his hand on his chest. "On the real."

Salmon laid his hand on the other man's shoulder. "Take it slow, Orrie. I'll get those things to Roe."

Eyes wet he said, "I feel bad putting you out. I --"

"Don't sweat it."

They looked at each other for several moments then Salmon gave the shoulder a gentle squeeze. He then turned and raised his hand at the CCTV camera mounted in one of the other corners of the room aimed at the bed. Thereafter the door sprang open and he said what might be his last good-bye to his friend. He dabbed a finger at his eye as he walked back along the hallway. Claudia the nurse was exiting a room containing several beds with patients.

"It was good you came to see him."

"I owe him."

"I hear you."

The guard behind the protected counter gave him the once over as he took off the badge and slid it through the slot. Salmon's personal items were returned to him, watch, wallet and car keys to the rental he was driving. Back outside he breathed in deep in the parking lot. Being inside those walls even as an official visitor had chilled him. Like a man trapped in a real life *Twilight Zone*, he'd flashed on being detained once he tried to leave. That a bogus charge had come across their computer screens with his picture and description attached. They were on alert, waiting to pounce. Guns pressed to his head as commands were screamed at him, he'd be proned out and hauled into the bowels of Sweetwater, behind bars yet again. Or maybe he was imaging a near future once he carried out why he'd been summoned.

Both men knowing the room was under watch, pictures and if desired sound, it wasn't a casual gesture when he was initially standing and put his hand on the hospital bed's railing. His back was blocking the camera's view and he'd asked Childress what was up using sign language. Or rather their modified form as there was prison slang mixed in. The older man indicated he'd sent a letter to a dead drop from the old days. There were a few other times during the visit they'd communicated this way like when Salmon stood and reached across for the water. But they'd kept their surreptitious "talking" to a minimum so as not to have the guards looking on, eyebrows raised.

All written communication from a prisoner was read first and so the letter itself would be in code. Too the dead drop was a street address and not a post office box as that would raise suspicions and the authorities could refuse to send it along.

Salmon didn't know what the job was, but he did know that if he ignored the dying man's plea, Orrie Childress' daughter and kids would be the ones to suffer. He dreaded returning to his old life and the possibility of being sent back to the joint. But he was jammed up. Orrie was not only his mentor of a sorts, if such could be said about professional thieves. But he'd saved his life on a job they were in on that went sideways when he was younger. The one in charge had double-crossed the crew and tried to kill them. Nor was Salmon a man to walk away when a friend was in trouble – though he doubted if Roe knew any of this. One of his few saving graces was Childress had assiduously kept his bent life away from his only child.

Back in his hotel room, he paced. Figuring he was going to be dragged into a situation flying out to Arizona to see Childress, he was using part of his stockpile of vacation days from the garage. Still, he owed it to call the man who'd given him a second chance. Yet still being cautious, he took out the Sat phone to make the call – the preferred hard to trace device of spies and drug dealers he wryly reminded himself.

"Is it that serious?" Archer Snow asked after he answered the call.

"I wanted you to have what you'd call plausible deniability, Arch. I have to honor a debt. But like the song says, it's one no honest man can pay."

The one on the other end of the line let those words linger. Finally, he said, "Since I know it's no good trying to talk you out of whatever this is, there must be something I can do to help."

"You can't."

"I still know how to stay in the background."

"Thanks, Arch. But this is the only time you'll be hearing from me like this. If in a week or so you don't see me coming through the garage's doors...well, if a cop should turn up and ask you what you know, you know nothing. We never had this conversation."

"You haven't told me anything," he emphasized.

"And we'll keep it that way."

Childress had several dead drops scattered about the West and Southwest. Most of the jobs he'd pulled had been in this region, though he'd also down scores in the South and the New York area. He'd burned through the cash he'd acquired over the years but had also plowed portions of those funds into legitimate businesses. One was an investment in a bar-be-cue joint called Mr. Jim's in Los Angeles' Crenshaw Distrust. An area of town that was still mostly black but a fair amount of Japanese Americans had also resided here. There was once a bowling alley on Crenshaw Boulevard called Holiday Bowl where various folks fraternized. These days a new light rail was coming in, bringing with it the encroachment of gentrification.

"YOU NEED NO TEETH TO EAT MY BEEF" was emblazoned on the building under Mr. Jim's unlit neon sign. The savory aroma of barbecued meat filled the restaurant's interior this afternoon.

Inside Salmon waited until the customer in front of him had placed their order. Off to the side sat a teenager intently watching his smartphone's screen. The big man stepped up to the order counter. "I believe you have a letter for Harold Isles," he said to the young lady who worked here.

"Who?" she said. Each of her long nails were finished in different designs.

"That's okay, Shawna, I'll take care of this." It was a woman in her thirties looking out through the rectangular opening onto the kitchen. She was cutting some ribs, a three-legged stool with a video controller on it near her. She removed her loose clear plastic gloves as she went deeper into the kitchen and in a few moments came through a set of swing doors, wiping her bare hands on a dish towel. She had the letter in a pocket on her sauce-stained apron. She took this out and handed it across to Salmon.

"Here you go, mister."

"Thanks."

"How is he?"

The woman wasn't Childress' daughter, but she seemed genuinely concerned. "He doesn't have long," he said quietly.

"Okay." She remained there a beat then returned to the kitchen.

Back outside, Salmon felt a tingle right where the back of his head and neck met. A familiar sensation that had him scanning his surroundings more than casually. He walked up the block then reversed course, paying particular attention to the parked cars. It had been the kid engrossed with his phone that had triggered the alarm in his head. The phone being a ubiquitous piece of high tech. Sweetwater was wired to the gills. Orrie isolated in a room. Yet when he was leaving, he'd seen the kind nurse exiting a room containing a man attached to machines as his friend was. Orrie had been alone to better hear what he had to say to him.

"Too long out of the game," he muttered, lamenting he was slipping. He got back in the car, smiling ruefully. This was the same rental he'd been driving in Arizona, intending to either fly back from the Southland or be buried here. A while later in his room at the hotel offering a view of the new futuristic-looking football venue, SoFi Stadium it was called, he read the letter. At first glance it was a message written from one old friend to another. Only there was no one named Harold Isles and the letter was written in code. The key to cracking the code was a book called the *Irish Isles*. This he knew from the clues Childress had told him. Salmon did not have a copy, but he knew where to find one.

Downstairs in the hotel's covered parking, he used a flashlight from the toolkit he'd brought with him. It didn't take too long to find the GPS tracker magnetically attached to the underside of the rental's rear wheel well. Clearly it had been placed there when he was at the prison. He left the device where it was. Back in the lobby, Salmon consulted google maps and saw there was a library less than two and a half miles away. Rather than summon a driver through a ride hailing app, he walked. He could use the exercise and more importantly, he could better tell if he was being tailed.

Salmon reached the library seemingly unincumbered. Inside he found the travel book first written in 1952. Facing outward to see anyone approaching, he sat at a table with pen and paper decoding the message. He read the words twice, committing pertinent facts to memory. Thereafter he returned the book to its proper place on the shelf. In the bathroom, making sure he was alone, he set the letter and decoded notes afire and let the sheets burn in the sink, then washed the ashes down the drain. The fire was small enough it hadn't set off the fire alarm or sprinklers. Walking back to the hotel he took a different route to see if he was being followed. He wasn't and he stopped at a Rite Aid to buy a few items including sewing thread and a glue stick.

Funny but as he walked out of the drugstore, it hit him being intent on finding out what Orrie had been involved in, he hadn't eaten breakfast. And he regretted not getting something to go from Mr. Jim's. There was a Denny's he'd passed on the way to the library and he stopped in there to get a late lunch.

"What'll you have?" the waitress asked him after he'd set aside the menu. He sat at the counter. She was a copper-colored woman, her hair done in Bohemian twists. Her stylish earrings gleamed. She was maybe a few years older than him, an alert face and a truckload of life behind her amber eyes.

"Let me get a Philly cheesesteak with everything on it and a lemonade."

"Fries?"

"Salad."

She glanced at him, making a pleasing sound in her throat. She sauntered away.

From what he gleaned from the letter, Childress had been brought in to essentially consult on a takedown. It had been planned nearly two months in advance and concerned a casino located in Southeast Los Angeles County in a town called Bell Park. Matters went haywire and the three-person crew assembled to pull the job went bust. One of them was caught and ratted out Orrie for a lighter sentence. The old man would have gotten away but by then the emphysema he'd been fighting back by sheer will to finish off this one last score, had gotten the best of him. He was dying so no need to run, he'd concluded.

The job's backer, the banker financing the overhead, Edgar Talmadge, expected Childress to put together another string and carry off the score. The old man was in no position to do so but he didn't like having this unfinished business hanging over his family. Talmadge might press his daughter to find his plans or who knew what, bringing them unwanted heat from the law. Salmon also understood the robbery had to take place during a specific window of time which was imminent.

"Here you go, handsome," the waitress said, setting down his drink order.

"Thank you."

Salmon knew of Talmadge from the old days, a stiff-necked bastard. He hadn't worked with him directly, but from other thieves had heard stories about him...none of them particularly flattering. If he was a different kind of reformed thief, he'd use a bullet to this chump's skull to settle the matter. But unlike some he'd known in this line of work, he couldn't kill in cold blood. He couldn't have that type of poisoned karma hanging over his head.

His food arrived and she set the plate down with a smile. He smiled back.

Good thing he reflected as he ate, he'd been on a few gnarly security gigs with Abraham Snow. Late on picking up the electronic surveillance meant he was out of step, but not that much. He had a known and unknown antagonists to deal with, and he better get up to speed so as not to get caught in the rundown. But like it or not, he had to contact Talmadge. Still first things first. After he finished his meal, he left a sizable tip and the waitress winked at him as he exited the restaurant. He didn't want to arouse suspicions and avoid using the rental, but he had to safeguard where he was next heading. He fetched the car and drove it in the opposite direction of where he wanted to be. The way he figured it, whoever was tracking him could afford to hang back so as to not be spotted. At any rate, he drove to a residential area and parked the car. He got out and walking along the street, went down a walkway of a modest apartment building. This let him out onto the carport off an alley. He walked along then climbed over a chain link fence. In this way he was now on another block. He used a burner he'd bought, a throwaway pre-paid cell phone, to summon a ride. In turn he was taken toward his destination. Yet ever cautious, he had the driver let him out a few blocks from his actual end point. He walked to a UPS store in a strip mall that contained mailboxes for rent.

Salmon had to wait until the two employees in there were busy at the dual service counter. Fortunately for him the mail boxes were in the corner of the store and not in direct eyesight of the counter. He didn't have a key, but the lock wasn't exactly up to Fort Knox specifications and he overcame it using his lockpicking tool. He extracted a thick 9x12 envelope and relocked the box. At that moment one of the employees rounded the corner, regarding him.

"Can I help you, sir?"

"No thanks, I've got it." He briefly shook the envelope at him, making no effort to hide the parcel.

"Very good." Still, he watched him as he exited.

He summoned another ride and went back to his car. He retraced his steps. If he was being surveilled live and in color, his tail might assume he'd gone to see a woman friend or who knows what. Salmon had tucked the envelope into the rear of his jeans' waistband under his loose T, as usual an unbuttoned plaid shirt over that. In the rental he drove back to the hotel. Upstairs in the hallway outside of his room, he bent down to see if the thread he'd attached to the door and the doorframe had been broken. Salmon had put out the Do Not Disturb doorhanger to keep housekeeping from entering. The thread was still attached, and he took this as a sign the room hadn't been entered and bugged.

At the desk he studied the contents of the envelope. Childress had done extensive notes of the target, a safe in the penthouse of the Phan-Tan Casino and Hotel in Bell Park. The casino was owned by the spry octogenarian Albert Dietz. Dietz was a billionaire given to supporting odd causes like a colony on Jupiter movement and a subscriber to various out there conspiracy theories. He had a foundation that distributed books and what have you on spiritual enlightenment. Like during the Cold War years and smuggling Bibles into the Soviet Union, the reading material was sent into authoritarian countries. In this way Dietz believed he was advancing human potential. He was a germaphobe and into psychic whorah as well. There was an apartment Dietz maintained off his penthouse office. He didn't live there fulltime but from what Orrie Childress had amassed, he was due to be back there in three days time. There was more pertinent information as well as hand drawn diagrams Childress had done of the office and its environs.

"You're a pro, old man," he muttered admiringly.

Salmon didn't feel comfortable keeping this valuable information in the room yet needed it to be nearby. There was as safe in the room and the hotel maintained a larger one downstairs. For several reasons he eschewed using either one of these. Down the hall was a compact cubby with an ice maker and vending machine. He had to wait as he heard muffled footfalls on the hall carpeting coming near. Salmon pretended to be deciding on a selection as a man in shorts went passed. Soon he heard the elevator doors dinging open and the stranger departing. The vending machine sat square to the tiled floor. He angled it away from the wall and stuck the plans behind it. He shoved it back in place.

Out on the street he took out his burner and made a call. The number memorized from Childress' letter.

"I'm going to install the windows." He then severed the connection.

For the time being he had to keep using his car. He retrieved his rental and drove it to a section of town he'd been to before when in L.A. last. This was an area called Venice, a trendy enclave of brew pubs and pilates studios near the ocean. He parked at a pay lot and using the burner again called a ride after walking a few blocks away. He was deposited at his destination, the Third Street Promenade in Santa Monica, its own city next door to where he'd parked. The Promenade was a pedestrian only corridor of retail shops, restaurants and movie theaters. He walked north to where the walkway, filled with locals and tourists out in the sun, ended at busy Wilshire Boulevard.

Waiting outside a shop at the corner selling fancy luggage and other travel items, a black Mercedes Maybach sedan with smoked windows pulled to the curb in front of him. The back door swung open automatically and Salmon got in. As if powered by dreams, the car silently moved away again into light traffic. They headed south. Skateboarders, joggers, people in business attire on motorized scooter and strollers traveled along the boardwalk fronting the rolling waves of the Pacific.

"I know you," Edgar Talmadge said. He was white, late fifties, coiffed mane of silver hair. He looked something like ex-Cowboys coach turned NFL broadcaster Jimmy Jones. He was shaking a finger at the other man, then snapped his finger. "Salmon, right?"

"Yeah."

"Of course, it would be you the old bird would bring in on this."

"You didn't leave him much choice."

His eyes flicked to the triangular back of the woman driving the car. That she was ex-military was evident to Salmon. In turn she was gauging Salmon in the rearview.

"You don't have to put extra bass in your voice, big man. This is just business."

A tension he hadn't been aware of subsided in his upper body. He settled onto the car's buttery leather. "I'll do the job but will need a few things. And your word that once done, you leave Orrie's family alone."

"Again, nobody's throwing around threats, Salmon."

Ignoring that he continued. "From what I understand, it's not money you want out of Dietz's safe."

"How do you know that? Orrie spill the beans, did he?"

"He's a pro and so am I. Nobody except him and us three are in the know."

"Make sure, huh?" he said sharply.

Salmon didn't take the verbal bait and remained silent.

Talmadge held up a hand. "Okay, look, it's just I've come this far and can't afford any slip ups."

"What am I getting out of the safe?"

"You mean what are you two getting."

"I don't need a babysitter. I can get anybody else I need."

The silver-haired man inclined his head. "And I need the reassurance you won't skip out on me, try to get revenge for your friend or some other version of a thief's warped sense of whatever." He laughed dismissively. "Kel is in on the takedown. Plain and simple. And don't underestimate her because she's a woman, she's aces under pressure. More than many men I know"

"I'll take your word for it," he said flatly.

"When is it going down?" the one called Kel asked from the driver's seat.

"I'm taking a gander out there today and will let you know." He held up a hand, anticipating Talmadege's remark. "I know the robbery has to happen when Dietz is back in his casino." Whatever it was, it meant Dietz was traveling with the thing.

"So, about the item?" he added.

"It's small"

"Huh?"

Talmadge leveled a hard stare at him. "Your job is to get what I say to get. The agreement I had with Childress was whatever money he retrieved, was his to keep. That crazy sumabitch Dietz is known to keep a few million on hand. As to what I want, the only thing you need to know it's probably a thumb drive, SD card or some other portable damn thing." Momentarily he looked out the window at a Hollywood beautiful young woman in a bikini top and cutoffs rollerblading along as if having no care in this troubled world.

Salmon doubted if it was a sex video. Though maybe it was Dietz in a session with a dominatrix and he was crawling around on the floor in giant diapers. He refocused. "I'm going to have a list once I get back from reconnoitering the place. But I already know some of the equipment I'll need."

Dismissively he said, "You and Kel can work that out."

Momentarily her face was in profile as she looked back at Salmon then put her hazel eyes back on the road.

Salmon didn't like the set-up one damn bit, but he was in it now. The only way out of thieves' alley was to make it to the other end. That evening after getting back from Bell Park and having his dinner at the Denny's, he learned the waitress was named Odetta. Thereafter Salmon returned to his room and made some initial notes. Putting those away, he relaxed, watching a classic boxing match on ESPN, the volume on low. This was the Erik Morales vs. Manny Pacquiao fight from 2005. As the Pac-Man tagged Morales with a swift jab, a soft knock sounded on the door.

"Yes," he called out.

"House security, Mr. Salmon," said an authoritative voice from the other side.

"Hold on." He got up and went to the peephole. Standing in front of his door was a smiling white guy with a crew cut. He opened the door but not all the way. The security man wore a sport coat over a polo shirt with a two-way clipped to his belt. He was six-two and stocky.

What can I do for you?" Salmon said.

"Well, sir, there's been a complaint."

"Really, against me?"

The security man glanced down the hallway then swived his head on his bull neck back at Salmon. "It would be better if we discussed this inside, don't you think?"

He grinned. "Sure, of course." He opened the door further, stepping aside slightly. A quiet roar escaped the boxing crowd on the television.

As the other man stepped into the room, he reached a hand under his coat and whipped around with a collapsible baton he unfurled with a flick of his wrist. He swiped it at Salmon who if he hadn't been anticipating an attack, would have been struck in the face and stunned. Instead, he brought his hand up deflecting the blow and countered with a punch to the fake security man's nose. He hit him hard, staggering the man. Salmon rushed forward the door slamming shut behind them. The other man recovered quicker than he'd hoped and this time he cracked the baton on Salmon's torso causing terrific pain. He reared back, knocking into the flatscreen, partially loosening it from the wall. Pacquiao was backing up Morales onto the ropes but the image flickered and switched to a nature program as the TV tilted.

The baton came up again as Salmon bent forward, the weapon striking him along the shoulder. But his momentum carried both of them onto the bed. There they grappled as the mattress slid, spilling them onto the floor. Salmon had a hold of the other's forearm, stopping another blow from striking him. He uppercutted the man, causing his teeth to clack. Back on his feet, Salmon tried to kick him but the other one grabbed Salmon's calf and twisted him aside. He too got to his feet and in a flurry of motion, they exchanged blows. On the crooked flatscreen, a hummingbird sucked nectar from a bright yellow flower.

The combatants were now on the other side of the bed where the desk and chair were. A standing lamp was knocked over, its heavy glass bursting with a dull pop. Salmon was hit in the stomach, but his hardened abdomen absorbed most of the blow. He countered and sent the other one into the chair. And this time when he aimed a foot at him, he connected right on the point of his chin. He got glassy-eyed and Salmon moved in to finish him off. He rained more punches to the other man's head and shoulders as he half-rose, knocking him and the chair over. The collapsible baton had rolled nearby. He scooped it up and after several vicious whacks with the thing, the other one was on all fours, blood dripping from his gaping mouth. Pulling his arm back like a major leaguer, salmon brought the baton down on the offered head and knocked the reeling man prone to the carpet.

Catching his breath, Salmon bent down and rolled the still man onto his back. Two fingers together on his neck, he checked the other's pulse. He was alive which meant he didn't have the problem of getting rid of a dead body. Then he went through his pockets finding no identification, not even car keys or a phone. Smart, he'd left any ID elsewhere, probably in the car he was driving which was no doubt stashed in hotel parking. He wasn't going to waste time looking for the vehicle. He was sure too this guy was connected to the tracer that had been put on his car. From the looks of him, Salmon figured he was one of the guards from Sweetbrook. Not simply rank and file but probably a captain. His burner didn't have picture capabilities and anyway, he wasn't going to concentrate on hunting down exactly who this chump was.

He left the man where he lay and packed his bags. Not hurriedly but moving efficiently. Salmon checked his appearance in the bathroom mirror, a welt on his face and a split knuckle but otherwise no other outward indications he'd just been on a fight. No sense tidying up the room either he concluded. Hippos cavorted in a lake on the television. When the other one had referred to him by his real name, that was a giveaway. He'd checked in under an assumed name and a counterfeit driver license and would check out using the same, making sure to pay for damages to lessen any inquiries about him. Nonetheless he wiped down the room of his prints as he'd always planned to do. There was though all sorts of trace DNA evidence around, but he calculated there would be no call for that sort of inspection. He checked the hallway, and it was clear. Using a fireman's carry, he took the moaning man into the stairwell. He descended three flights and dumped him in that hallway. He was coming around, so he socked him again and departed. Salmon was on the road less than twenty minutes later, having left the GPS tracker behind.

Where the 5 and 710 freeways intersected in this part of Los Angeles county were off ramps on each throughway for Bell Park. The municipality was 5.4 square miles, home to several fulfillment warehouses, truck yards, battery plants, and even a slaughterhouse called Farmland where some 6,000 pigs were processed daily the euphemism went. The stench surrounding the place was unremitting and birds constantly circled overhead or perched on its roof.

These businesses represented the majority of the jobs aside from the public institutions. There was a fire department and a part-time city council with a full-time city manager and staff representing the workings of the local government. The small town also had its own police force. The residential sections were mostly older housing stock, Craftsmen, California bungalow, Spanish Mediterranean and even a few McMansions.

Salmon soon arrived back at the Phan-Tan Casino and Hotel complex. The establishment was constructed from the old Atlas Tire and Rubber factory originally built in the last century in 1930. Once upon a time it was the largest such entity west of the Mississippi. The façade was patterned after the palace of the ancient Assyrian King Sargon the Second. Details such as winged bulls with human heads and numerous other ornate mythical designs were inscribed on the outer and inner walls of the place. Parking was free and the large lot was filled with older model cars and pick-up trucks, several big rigs as well. People came from as far away as Riverside and San Diego to try their luck at the Phan-Tan.

The interior was the usual array of slot machines operated by mostly old timers, some with walkers nearby and others with their portable oxygen generators draped over their torsos. They vigorously played the one arm bandits. Waitresses in skimpy outfits moved fluidly in and around the machines with drink trays. Childress' diagrams included Dietz's penthouse and the location of the hidden built-in safe. There was also a panic room up there containing a direct trunk line to the police department.

As the numbers on the safe's electronic pad were changed regularly, there was no combination to be had. No sense making it too easy Salmon had considered when he was studying the diagrams again in a rear booth at the Denny's last night. Walking around the casino, Salmon had been weighing vague notions of a plan driving out here, but he didn't think he was about to try and get on the roof and work his way down on a cable to the office. That would require too many specialty tools as well as more personnel in pulling the job. As it was, he was saddled with Kel Monroe, Talmadge's all-purpose enforcer it seemed.

Eventually he took up residence on a stool nursing a beer in the casino's main bar, the Diamond Head.

"Hey, man, get the hell off me," a voice rose over the din of active gambling.

Salmon and several others looked over to see two security guards on either side of a whiskered individual wearing a baseball cap and quilted vest. He was clutching a bunch of chips and cash to his chest, some spilling onto the ground as he was forced toward the door.

"My money's as good as everyone else in this snake pit," the man said.

"That don't give you license to grope the waitresses, asshole," one of the guards said.

"Aw, I was just being friendly."

They finished escorting him out of the place. The guards were trim and in-shape, their uniforms crisply maintained. At their hips were sheathed pepper spray canisters, T-handle batons and sidearms. From Orrie's notes he knew Dietz's guard force weren't a bunch of minimum wage schlubs but earned pretty decent pay and were expected to act with decorum and be professional. One more threat to be neutralized Salmon catalogued. He finished his beer and wandered around more, making sure to gamble so as not to draw attention as if he was casing the joint -- which he was.

"Bust," said the dealer of his own hand as he turned over a nine at the Blackjack table.

"I know when to fold 'em," Salmon said, getting up from the table. He'd parlayed a ten of hearts and a joker, a wild card in California casinos, to see the win. This after a better than average run over the last forty minutes.

"What's your hurry, big boy?" an older Chinese American woman with a gold tooth said to him three chairs over.

She wasn't bad looking, but he wasn't fooled. He knew a shark when he saw one. He left her a chip and winking, went to one of the cashier's cages to get his money. It was a check for four hundred and forty dollars. Toward the rear of the split-level room there was the kitchen. In there he recalled from the notes was a private elevator that serviced the upper levels. Of course, operating the elevator required a pass code. Only the chef and the sous chef knew it. Still he wanted to take a look in there. Sitting at one of the slot machines, he ordered a vodka so as to have liquor on his breath. In no hurry, he drank and played then got up and headed toward the kitchen.

In there the staff was busy with their tasks and for a few moments he wasn't noticed. He went down one pathway between hanging pots and the like and turning a corner, came to an inset area where the elevator was located. He got close, his back to the workers.

"Hey, homey, you can't be back here."

"Wha?" Salmon said, turning, fumbling with his phone as if trying to talk on it. "Gotta call Elmira and tell her about the good news," he said, putting on a drunk act, weaving some but not overdoing it. Making sure to also breath in the sous chef's face.

"Okay," said the shorter man, a Chicano in cook's gear with an earring and a handkerchief tied around his head. He put a firm hand on Salmon's shoulder. "This way, brah, and you can tell your girl all about it."

"Yeah, sure, no worries, chief. Say, you 'member Elmira's number?" He leaned into the guy and was removed from the kitchen.

He went out the way he came in but didn't return to his car. Salmon walked around the perimeter, scanning the exteriors of the building. The layout of the 8-story hotel overlooked the 2-story casino, the two structures as seen from the side an 'L' shape. The kitchen he'd been in was deep enough in that the elevator he'd spied was contained within the taller building. Dietz's penthouse of living quarters and office commanding the top floor of the hotel. It was built like a pill box dropped on top, as there was also a rooftop garden area up there as well. The casino and hotel were on their own concrete pad of an island, no other buildings nearby as tall as the hotel, which was small by Vegas standards. Salmon's was sure he wasn't going to execute the break-in on Dietz's office from above, but he wanted to double-check.

Consulting google maps, Salmon drove to the sole public library branch in town. He used a computer there and called up articles and news reports about the town's patriarch. He wanted more details about Dietz. In particular he was interested in the man's superstitions on top of his germophobic tendencies. He was forming the idea one or both of these aspects of his personality could be exploited to his benefit.

"I don't consider myself unduly pre-occupied with cleanliness," Dietz was saying in a taped interview from several years ago. "The Swine flu, ebola, Sars, and who knows what all else will be floating in the air at us. Being vigilant with one's body, and I'm nobody's kid, doesn't that make sense in this world of ours where people come and go from this region or that area on a daily basis?" Dietz was sitting in a wing chair in a suit, no tie. His legs were crossed and he looked calm and composed. He was in his late seventies when this was taped, but looked fit for his age, grey hair close on his head and his face lean, eyes alert.

"This is not just me being self-absorbed," he continued. "In my casino we have a state-of-the-art air filtration system and various sanitizing stations throughout. And of course in the kitchen we maintain the highest standards of cleanliness and staff is regularly sanitizing the surfaces with medicated wipes."

At one point the offscreen interviewer asked, "What about your belief in the other wordly let's call it."

Dietz laughed easily. "Just as I consult my economic advisors regarding how my money is doing, or see a therapist to help me in times of psychological stress, I also consult those who provide guidance in terms of spiritual well-being." On he went, Salmon paying close attention. Post the interview he scanned through other articles about the man. He found a passage in a local throwaway newspaper. It read in part, "It's known that when Albert Dietz is staying in town, he calls upon the services of a local psychic who goes by Lady Sylvia. She's a Bell Park native and court records indicate her full name is Sylvia Zendajas."

Salmon sat back, absorbing this, the plan crystalizing. He leaned forward again. Using the computer, he found the address for Lady Sylvia who advertised her all-seeing abilities, and rates. He made a note of her address and closed down the computer. Strolling away from the library he made a call. Through his connection to Snow Security Consulting, and particularly as Archer Snow was an ex-operative, Salmon was privy to contacts who specialized in certain skill sets, including ones who devised electronic bugging devices. The line clicked on but no voice was heard. He expected this. He also knew the call had been answered by a machine that would bounce the signal around to hide the source point of his call.

"This is John Salmon. I'm calling you from a burner that I will soon dispose of. I need a referral." He hung up and returned to his car. It was a gamble he wasn't being watched personally at the moment, but time was not on his side. He had to not only be about putting all the pieces together but operating as safe as he could given the limitations imposed on him.

Kel Monroe wore stylish slacks and a silky top. Her hair was combed differently, she had in hoop earrings and had on more makeup that she normally wore. Which was to say she normally didn't wear any. She knocked on the security screen of the modest well-kept house located on a street not too far from the Farmland slaughterhouse. Close enough that its silhouette was visible over the rooftops, but far enough away its particular aroma wasn't apparent. The lawn of the house was neat and green and on it was a sandwich board sign announcing this was where Lady Sylvia offered her supernatural services.

"Yes," said an older voice from within. The security screen was painted white and could not been seen through.

"Hi, I'm Terri," the disguised Monroe said.

"Oh yes, dear, do come in."

The screen was unlocked and Monroe stepped inside a front room decorated in muted tones with various sort of mystic-looking bric-a-brac about including a medium-sized gargoyle perched on the fireplace's mantle. Surprisingly there wasn't a table with a cloth and crystal ball on it. Rather there was an alcove off the front room containing two comfortable leather club chairs canted at an angle to each other. There was a built-in bookcase behind this, the whole of it suggesting a psychiatrist's décor rather than that of a soothsayer. There was even a teacart off to one side with cups, saucers and a teapot on it.

"Thank you so much for seeing me, Lady Sylvia."

"I could fit you today as tomorrow, well, let's just say I always need to set aside the whole day for Mr. Deitz when he's in town." Lady Sylvia was a handsome stocky woman whose veined hands were evidence of someone who'd not always worked the spiritualist hustle.

Monroe held back a smirk at the older women leveling a humble brag. She went into her act, sniffling and touching the corner of her eye with an already damp handkerchief from her purse. "Oh, Lady Sylvia, I thought Harold was the man for me. A true soulmate. But now…" she trailed off as if her next words were too dreadful to voice.

"Come my dear, sit and let me see if I might guide you to a solution to your vexing problem."

"Oh, thank you, thank you."

They retreated to the alcove and Monroe as Terri told Lady Sylvia her made up tale of woe, making sure to pause now and then, overcome with grief.

"I hope that bullshit I went through was worth it," she groused the next day. She and Salmon sat in his new motel room in Bell Park. It was the '60s era Wayfarer Inn offering a buffet lunch employees from the slaughterhouse and the traveling truckers who stayed there dined at regularly. They were listening on a portable monitor to the bugging device Monroe had planted in the alcove. Dietz had arrived and after pleasantries was now in session with Lady Sylvia. The electronic gear was among the equipment Monroe had obtained from his contact's referral.

"Whatever we can use to our advantage," he said.

She huffed and had more of her chai latte.

The minutes dragged on and so far Salmon hadn't heard anything much different than what he'd heard on the interview at the library. Monroe made no effort at hiding her boredom. Finally, the conversation got interesting.

"I've come into possession of what might be advantageous to me or a bomb that will go off in my hands. I have trepidations about wielding this information. But I also knew I didn't want to do anything one way or the other until I consulted you."

"You flatter me, Albert. As you know, I don't advise you on the minutia of your varied interests, but rather I attempt to foresee an outcome that advances your well-being, your cosmic balance appropriately."

"Lay it on a little thick why don't you," Monroe quipped.

Salmon pointed at the monitor signaling for her to pay attention. She gave him the bug eyes.

Dietz was saying, "This is only known to you and me, Lady Sylvia. Only you can proffer guidance in this regard. I know if I were to make this information known, much in the way of adversity would be leveled at me in terms of the courts and possibly beyond legal backlash."

"Then you should walk away if this matter vexes you so."

"But you know me," he retorted.

"Not all challenges are meant to be taken head on."

"Yes, yes that is so. But I'm very inclined to take the risk. The rewards are that high."

"You mean money, Albert? You have more than enough," his spiritual advisor said.

"No. I don't mean materially. With your able wisdom supplied over the years those are not my concerns. If what I have in hand is true, I'm talking about not fame, but my legacy. Being seen as more than just some crazy recluse with a second-rate casino." He chuckled.

"But this...device if realized could be used for good but how well I know the history of this country. War upon war, death and destruction. I just don't know. Look what Pandora released," he said wistfully.

Monroe and Salmon exchanged a look. "Is he going to say what the hell he's talking about or keep being cryptic?" he said.

Monroe's face was unreadable.

They kept listening but Dietz never came right out and said what it was he possessed, what it was he and Monroe were going to steal and turn over to Talmadge. Though he did say the information had come into his possession through his foundation. His people had developed sophisticated methods of smuggling hard copies and electronic files

"And a good man paid the price for smuggling it out," he added.

At one point Monroe crossed her arms, focused inward Salmon observed.

The day of the robbery Salmon and Monroe entered the Phan-Tan hotel lobby dressed casually. The day was overcast and both wore stylish light windbreakers. They rode up to the seventh floor, floor eight being locked off to the public where operations was as well as the penthouse above that floor. Once in the hallway, the two walked along with another person who'd gotten off the elevator. They went past them as this woman paused at a door to use her key card. They'd chosen this time of day knowing the cleaning staff were still on their rounds but on the lower floors. Part of the information Childress had amassed.

Guided by the diagrams committed to memory, Salmon followed by Monroe rounded three corners to come to a dead end. This brought them to the door for the electrical switch room. In there was the various relays and apparatuses, including a computer, controlling dissemination of power from the basement power plant to the hotel's rooms and casino. For their purposes, there was also a cooling system to prevent overheating. This included an air vent. Not large enough to crawl into but large enough for their purposes. Salmon overcame the lock and both thieves stepped inside, closing the door behind them. They now wore supple gloves.

Wordlessly, he removed a section of a canister from his toolbox. Monroe did the same and they screwed the two halves together. Salmon removed a slim soft-sided kit from a hidden inner pocket of his windbreaker. He unzipped this and taking out a few slim instruments, went to work at a bank of blinking lights and toggle switches.

"I'm impressed," Monroe said.

"Thievery in the 21st century means being versed with electronics and their schematics," he said. After a few minutes he said, "Okay, I've reversed the fans."

Monroe nodded and attached a rubber tube to a nozzle atop the canister. She opened a valve and having inserted the end of the tube into the grill of the air ventilator in the wall, released the gas in the canister. The stuff was a harmless compound. But it gave off a noxious odor and was greenish in color-- meant to be seen and smelled.

"Okay, it's empty," Monroe announced, taking the canister apart and putting the halves away in the toolboxes. Salmon had already put his kit away and they stepped back into the hallway.

"Are you the electricians?" a middle-aged woman in business attire said from behind them. "The light in my bathroom isn't working. Right over the toilet I want you to know," she huffed.

"Ma'am, we're kinda busy with a matter right now," Salmon began. "I'll send somebody up to change the bulb."

"Oh, you're too damn important to deal with my little problem is it?" She leaned toward them. "You know, you two aren't dressed like electricians. What are you two up to, hmmm? Maybe I should be the one calling downstairs."

She spun on her heel and Monroe covered the distance in a bound.

"Oh goodness me, what, what are you up to?" she said as Monroe got an arm around her neck. She was about to scream but she clamped a hand over her mouth too. With her other hand, she pressed two stiffened fingers on a particular nerve in her neck, putting her to sleep.

"Damn, just like Spock," Salmon commented.

"Come on, Gene Roddenberry, help me out here." Together they carried the unconscious woman back to her room, the door ajar in the short hallway. Salmon checked his watch as both used lamp chord to bind the woman and a torn scrap from a pillowcase to gag her.

"Second phase," Salmon announced when they'd finished. Calmly, they laid the woman on her back on the bed. Taking a seat on the edge of the bed, Salmon made a call from his burner. This was to an inner number into Dietz's office. A number retrieved by Talmadge obtaining Lady Sylvia's smartphones records at his request. Should anyone want to call him back, they'd reach a busy signal.

"Hello, hello," he said in an officious voice when the line was picked up. "This is Josh Morris from city water calling. Who do I have the pleasure of speaking too?"

"This is Frank Garris. What's going on? There's a terrible small and some kind of gas up here." Garris was one of Dietz's personal bodyguards. The other was named Whittaker.

"Yes, well, Mr. Garris there's been some sort of underground explosion and at this moment we're trying to determine not only the cause, but the nature of the chemicals released. It doesn't appear to have been methane but don't quote me on that, okay?" He added a nervous laugh then went on. "We're contacting those in the area and started with the casino and hotel, what with Mr. Dietz's stature here in Bell Park being a major employer."

"Should we evacuate?" Garris said.

"No, in fact we want everyone to shelter in place. It's our belief the gas is even now dissipating, though I'm getting reports there's a lingering presence of it on the street level so there may be some issuance of it from the source. Of course, everyone's safety is our paramount concern." He could hear Garris talking to whoever else was in the office and he then came back on the line.

"Very good. Thanks for calling."

"Of course." Salmon hung up and he and Monroe left the room. The woman on the bed stirred, moaning slightly.

Downstairs in the casino, maters proceeded as normal. So when the two with hand held devices in hard hats and coveralls showed up and went to the locked off service elevator in the kitchen, they were stopped.

"You can call my boss if you want," a disguised Salmon said. Both he and Monroe carried their toolboxes.

"I'm'a call upstairs first," the chef said. He did and what he heard confused him. "We haven't smelled anything down here," he said to Garris. But these guys say they need to take readings up there."

"The boss says let 'em up."

Salmon had counted on Dietz's fear of germs to override any security concerns.

"Okay." The chief unlocked the elevator and up the two thieves went. Each put on a mask. These were plasticine-like thin membranes that adhered to their skin. Dead white, the masks gave them an otherworldly quality. Particularly as contrasted against Salmon's darker hue. The rubber gloves they slipped on were black and form-fitting. Both thieves knew there were various cameras deployed throughout the penthouse. But there was no monitoring station downstairs for them. They were designed to record from up top. There was a monitor board in the panic room. Dietz valued his privacy. The penthouse was well-insulated, cutting down on noise escaping Salmon had also noted.

The elevator reached the penthouse and the door dinged open. Garris in shirt sleeves was standing there and instantly reacted at seeing individuals in masks. He reached for his gun which was holstered in the small of his back.

"Intruders," the bodyguard yelled.

Monroe executed a martial arts kick to clip Garris, but he too was versed in close combat skills as his file had indicated. He leveled his semi-automatic to blast her, but Salmon went into action. He threw a mini smoke grenade laced with the stuff in pepper spray.

"Shit," he blarcd, blindly firing his gun.

Salmon had moved in under the gunfire and with a one-two combination, rocked Garris. And this time when Monroe brought her leg up high, whipping it around in a blur, her foot struck the side of Garris' head. He dropped to the floor hard. Salmon then zip tied his legs and arms. By now though Whittaker had taken Dietz into the panic room. A move Salmon had accounted for in his plan.

Inside the panic room Dietz had Whittaker activate the direct alarm to the police department.

"They're pros, that's for sure," Whittaker said to his boss as the two regarded what was happening outside their secure rooms on the multi view screens. "But the police will get them before than can breach the safe."

"I hope so." Dietz pointed at one of the screens. On it, the white-faced Salmon could be seen securing Garris.

Minutes before Garris was secured, the dispatcher in the Bell Park police headquarters received the alarm from the panic room. Just as she tabbed her mic to send out patrol cars, a fusillade from machine guns blasted the station house, rounds embedding in its cinder block walls and spiderwebbing the bullet resistant glass.

"We're under attack," a uniform yelled as even more gunfire was unleashed on them.

Outside a parked empty patrol car was strafed from above and the gas tank sparked. The car blew up, the rear lifting off the ground, the burning wreck flipping over onto its top. A motorcycle cop wearing aviator shades was riding up and had to apply his brakes quickly to avoid flying flaming debris. The bike went out from under him and as it skidded into another parked patrol car. The officer also skidded to a stop, his helmeted head banging against a fire hydrant. He was knocked out cold.

"Drones, goddamn drones are buzzing us," another uniform announced, craning his neck as he dared looking out a window into the sky. The three cars out on patrol were called back to the station to help deal with the threat. Answering the alarm from the Phan-Tan Casino and Hotel would have to wait.

Back in the penthouse Salmon, who'd gotten the idea for using drones as a distraction after visiting Childress at Sweetbrook, attached two different hand-held devices by their magnetic bases to the face of the safe. It was large and hidden behind a section of wall. He then inserted a heavy wire each into the other, hardwiring them together. Both devices had a readout screen and he tapped their keypads as the sets worked in concert, hacking the safe's computer-controlled combination. Similar types of gadgets could be found if you knew where to look on the Dark Web -- along with quite a few knockoffs that didn't function properly. Orrie Childress had built these. Monroe looked on.

"Here we go," Salmon announced as a melodic tone sounded from the boxes. He opened the safe door. There were banded piles of cash, documents and more inside. There was also a small metal box. Salmon reached for this and opened it revealing several thumb drives. He also liberated some of the cash.

"Let's get out of here."

"You're not taking all the money?" Monroe asked.

"It's not for me." He crouched down, putting the cash in the toolbox.

"Shit," Monroe said, looking past Salmon and pulling her handgun free. Before she cleared her weapon, Whittaker shot her, and she fell back.

Salmon dove, getting the thick steel door between him and the bodyguard who continued firing. Momentarily protected, he rolled a mini flash bang grenade he'd also brought along in the toolbox. It went off with a white blinding light and a thunderclap of a boom. Prepared, Salmon had closed his eyes. He wasn't blinded as the other man was though his ears rang. Less disoriented, he reached out and took Monroe's gun lying on the floor, a bullet singeing his arm. He shot twice, striking Whittaker in his lower legs. He buckled and Salmon was on him, clubbing his head with the butt of the handgun several times until he lay still. He secured his hands then turned his attention to his wounded partner.

"So much for not leaving DNA evidence around," he said as he got an arm under her and to her feet.

"The bathroom," she breathed.

"Right," he responded, understanding. Leaving her leaning and leaking, he soon returned from hurrying in there.

"Leave it to a germaphobe to have this on hand," he said joyfully.

It was a commercial bottle of bleach spray and he liberally squirted the stuff on the blood stains on the carpet and where red had decorated the furniture. Meanwhile Monroe had pressed a torn piece of her shirt underneath her overalls to the wound in her side. Tossing aside the bottle, down the elevator they went. Fortunately for them it was designed to reach the basement where the power plant was located. This was also where service vehicles and the like could enter.

From a nearby trash receptacle Salmon found a torn swath of plastic wrapping and handed this to Monroe. She switched out the bloody cloth to press onto her wound. He put the cloth in the toolbox.

He said, "Stay here and I'll get the car."

"I won't be running away," she said wincing.

He trotted off carrying both toolboxes.

Agonizing minutes went by. Monroe breathed shallowly, leaning against a pillar, partially in shadow. The only footfalls down here belonged to employees and repair people. A few spotted her but kept to their own as she smiled, pretending to be waiting for something or another. A siren sounded in the distance, the drones having ceased attacking the police station. They'd been programmed to explode in the air to prevent being traced.

Salmon arrived with the sedan and she managed to get in unaided. Her side though was soaked in blood. He'd removed his overalls.

"You know anybody who can patch you up? Maybe a veterinarian?" He asked her as he calmly drove up the ramp and out into the sunshine. He knew of such people back home but not out here.

Monroe had a pained expression on her sweating face, her head pressed to the headrest. The gun was in her hand, laying on her stomach, pointed at him. He hadn't noticed her picking it up.

"I'm a federal agent, Salmon."

"I figured something was up," he drawled. "You seemed to know what Dietz had gotten hold of." He paused then, "Guess that means you don't have to sweat me dropping you off at a hospital."

"You seem pretty cool about this."

"I've been caught before," he said resignedly. "You weren't sent in undercover to bust Talmadge over back taxes."

"That's right." The car dipped going over a pothole and her right eye pinched closed.

"Now what?"

"There's a clinic in Cudahy you can get me to. Me and the thumb drives."

"What about Talmadge?"

"He'll get his."

"Eventually you mean. I have to make sure he doesn't go after Orrie's family."

"I won't lie to you, Salmon. You're an upright, guy. I believe you when you said the money was for someone else. But my mission remains what's on one of those drives. National security."

"Yeah," he said wistfully. "I hear you." He swerved the car viciously causing her to lurch forward. He clipped Monroe's temple with his elbow, stunning her. A right to the jaw put the weakened woman out. He made a call on his burner to the individual he'd obtained the bugging equipment from, leaving a message.

Later Monroe awoke on a gurney being wheeled into the emergency room. The police were informed as the law demanded reporting all gunshot victims. Her identification was fake, consistent with her Kel Monroe cover. She was eventually able to provide her bona fides post surgery and the successful removal of the bullet. The pertinent thumb drive was messengered in a coin-sized envelope to her bedside a day later. The acronym of the agency she worked for was not the FBI, the CIA or even the NSA. She and her superiors weren't concerned about going after John Salmon. The agent had gotten what she'd came for. She was pretty sure Salmon would obtain what he'd come for as well.

"If you as so much as breath in the direction of Orrie's daughter and kids, the North Koreans will find out you're in possession of the instructions detailing how to make Dr. Ri's force field prototype. What Dear Leader did to his half-brother in that airport will probably be a warm-up compared to what they'll do to you." He referred to an assassination using VX nerve compound that killed the half-brother almost instantly in the middle of the day.

Talmadge glared at him from behind his desk. "You got some balls, Salmon."

"You damn right I do." From where he stood in front of the buttoned-down gangster in the corner office, he flipped the copy of the thumb drive onto his desk's shiny surface. "You should know too Monroe is a fed. Might be kind of tough selling that on the black market now. Fact, you might want to get out of Dodge."

Once the encrypted file was cracked, Salmon made sure this copy was bereft of pertinent data. The complete original had gone to Monroe. He turned and walked out as the other man cursed at his back. The big man had a date to keep with a certain waitress, a last visit to make, then he too was going to get the hell out of here to get back home.

###

From his electronic bugging contact Salmon was introduced to a hacker. This goth dressing, gum chewing Antifa leaning young woman who went by the name Raincrow with more piercings than tatts had traveled to Bell Park to control the drones. She'd accomplished this hunkered down in an empty third floor apartment not too far away from the police station. He'd taken the cash to pay her for a job well done. He also paid her to hack into the Sweetbrook computer, ID'ing the fake security man who'd jumped him. He couldn't prove it, but Salmon was certain he must have been in cahoots with the warden at the prison. Their angle was to rob the robbers of Dietz's millions he concluded. When they tumbled he'd made them, they improvised. Probably figured to work him over until he told him what he knew and his plan. He could prove none of this, but it didn't sit right with him, crooked as they were.

Knowing this he still needed to ease Orrie Childress' mind, let him go out knowing he'd done right by his family. Making the arrangements, he drove back to Arizona. Though his heart thudded in his throat, he came and went at the prison unmolested. Guess it didn't hurt he'd had Raincrow send very specific text message to the guard and the warden.

In his hospital room at Sweetbrook maximum security prison, Orrie Childress finally succumbed. He'd been daydreaming of he and Miz Raquel walking hand-in-hand on a fluffy cloud. He died with a smile on his face.

The End.

BEN BOOKS PRESENTS...

The note appeared in her mailbox on a bright and sunny Monday afternoon. At first, Laura Snow didn't notice it. It hid amongst the other grouping of bills, credit card offers, and advertisement postcards. She slapped the lot of them down on the kitchen island and washed her hands in the sink. A turkey sandwich with mayo and bacon waited on the round table. She sat down and took a bite into the soft bread, noting again how much she loved the New Mexican bakery. The fresh made bread included the state's best-known export—green chiles.

When she'd eaten about half of her sandwich, her cellphone rang. She peeked over at the number and name.

Restricted.

She hurried, swallowed, and answered on the third ring, prepared to admonish the telemarketer.

"Look, my number is on the no contact list…"

"Laura." Archer's gravel voice sounded worn down by time, eroded with age.

"Hiya Archer."

So, not a telemarketer.

She knew her former father-in-law better. Despite being 70 years old, Archer Snow had the strength, energy, and stamina of men more than half his age.

"How's my boy?" Laura put down her sandwich and wiped her hands with a napkin. Her middle son, Abraham, had a passion for danger and knack for trouble. Something her former father-in-law exploited. The two were cut from the same cloth. "Is he doing okay?"

"Oh yeah. I did wanna touch base with you and let you know he's doing alright. He mentioned the other day he ain't heard from you."

The unspoken rebuke confirmed she made the right choice in putting her sandwich down.

"I see. Well, I've been a bit busy here, and I never know what you got him doing. Sometimes he can talk to me and sometimes he can't." Laura didn't want to re-tread this ground again, but Archer started it. "I'm glad he's safe and well."

Archer sighed as if he didn't want to go there either. "Yeah. He's a good kid…"

"I know. He's my son."

"I just thought I'd call you first."

"I appreciate it."

"You take care, Laura." His tone lightened and she could hear his smile.

"You, too. Watch out for him. Will you?"

"Always do."

After he hung up, Laura resumed eating lunch. On the small hutch beside the table framed photos of her children watched—two boys and one girl, now two men and one woman. They stood in birth order in every picture—Douglas, Abraham, and Samantha. They were the most beautiful things to come from such an ugly relationship with her ex-husband, their father, Dominic. Laura had long since removed all images of him, and at the thought of him, she choked.

Sputtering, she shot off the chair and raced to the kitchen. She snatched a glass from the drainage board and filled it with water. As she drank, she closed her eyes and swore that Dominic Snow had negative energy around him. She wouldn't invoke his name again. While one hand gripped the glass, her other hand reached for the crystal hanging around her neck. As her fingers closed over it, a calm draped over her, centering her in the here and now, and not the past.

Laura Snow, you are here, in Taos, New Mexico. Focus. You're right here. Home.

She opened her eyes and placed the now empty glass in the sink. Laura cleaned up her lunch area, putting the plate in the sink, and tossing her napkin away. Her separation and divorce from someone she had been in love with could be mind boggling. Who was she beyond Mrs. Snow? The breakdown of her marriage changed her—for the better. It forced her to rediscover her true self. It required careful excavation of herself. As she wiped down the counters, something blue caught her eye among the stack of mail and halted her musings.

"What's this? Probably some attempt to get me to buy something else I don't need." She flipped through a few envelopes and found the eye-catching mail.

It had a return address from Orlando, Florida, but the postal stamp read Albuquerque. Odd, but it was addressed to her in a black calligraphy styled script.

"Fancy." She chuckled, but despite the address there wasn't a name or business noted. She flipped it over to see if the sender put their name on the back.

Nope.

Intrigued, she got her letter opener from the island's drawer and sliced open the envelope. She took the letter out expecting it to be a marketing ploy or another attempt to get her to renew her car's warranty.

Instead, it contained exactly four words.

You. Will. Pay. Bitch.

Laura stared at the words, mouth agape. She'd been called worse, but why would someone send this to her? She picked up the envelope again, and sure enough, it was addressed to her. She hadn't misread it. When she went back to the letter, she checked the back for anything like notes, a P.S., but nothing. It hadn't been handwritten but printed out. No signature. The large size words were in what she liked to call the Halloween font.

The hairs on her neck went up and she dropped the letter onto the island. She grabbed her tall, kitchen trash can and swept the entire lot into the garbage. As she washed her hands at the sink, she looked out the window and out into her backyard. The warm water failed to chase the chill away.

Why would someone want me to pay? And for what? Was this some spurned lover having a laugh? Some silly joke from Dominic, maybe? Nah. Not his style.

This home hadn't been cheap, well nothing came that way in Taos. But the view was gorgeous. Crisp blue sky and in the spring and summer, her trees and those beyond turned green. Her one-level adobe, pueblo-styled home had exposed beams and beige walls. The sandstone tiles meant easy clean up when Chip had an accident. The beautiful inside had nothing on the outside. Her house sat on 1.40 acres and covered 2059 square feet. She could see the mountains in the distance, but close enough she could almost touch them. The property came with a hot tub so she could sit and listen to the wild and relax among the chilly nights. Her property also came with a pond, surrounded by trees.

Across her backyard, she spied the mountains and rolling hills of the Sandias. She loved living in Taos, and she enjoyed the pueblos, the food, the winters, the cool summers, and independence she gained here. Her home allowed her to have peace and be able to meditate and connect with nature. These tasks healed her soul.

A *bark* broke through her musings.

Chipotle nudged her hand and lifted those big brown eyes to her.

"You're right, Chip. It's after lunch. Time for a walk." She pushed the letter out of her mind and headed toward her back door. Once Laura got the leash on, Chip, short for Chipotle, stood at the door, her tag wagging. Laura pulled on her light jacket, grabbed her cell phone, and started out for an afternoon walk. The breeze chilled her, and she zipped her jacket all the way to her neck.

Once, she shut the door, Chip walked ahead, tugging a bit on the leash.

"No, not yet." Laura scolded.

Chip liked to run, her little legs pushing as fast as she could go. Something about the mountain air and the elevation set her 10-year-old Pomeranian to miniature racehorse.

Once they reached the pond, Laura removed the leash and let her run around a bit. Coming in at a whole 8 pounds, Chip acted like she derived from a full bloodied Rottweiler instead of a fluffy Pomeranian, but size didn't mean much and definitely didn't indicate a person—or dog's—courage.

Laura stood beside the dark waters, watching Chip chase birds nestled in the trees. Her closest neighbor lived over a mile away. Birds chirped. Furry animals scurried. The spring day unfurled.

A niggling in the back of Laura's head kept her from enjoying the beautiful day, like a shadow threatening to overtake the sunlight. A chill she couldn't repress. Chip halted, turned to Laura and barked, as if sensing her distress.

"I'm being paranoid." Her fingers found her crystal. The letter had disconcerted her.

"Fine. You win." Laura started to jog. Chip barked in joy and ran too.

At 57 years old, she didn't have a graceful run, but her legs still worked, and her lungs didn't collapse. She counted that as win. The two of them—seasoned owner and seasoned dog—ran along the makeshift trail around the expansive backyard.

A breeze flowed over her, and she pushed ahead in an attempt to leave the dark feeling behind her.

###

Two weeks later

Laura strolled into the art room on a sunny Tuesday morning.

Hector waved. "Hola."

"Hola. Commo est a?" Laura sat at her usual spot next to Hector and removed her paint brushes from their cases.

Hector tipped his hat. "Like I was telling Maggie, this new place got good sopapillas."

"Now, I'm intrigued." Laura dripped her brush in the purple paint. Hector flirted with all the women in their art circle. He bragged about his painting skills. "What's the restaurant's name, again?"

"Maria's Kitchen."

"He's been going on about it since he got here. Let's go there for our weekly lunch date." Maggie sat to Laura's left. She didn't dress appropriately for her age and Laura loved her for her live for the moment attitude.

The Taos Mature Painters Club were a tight-knit group. Laura sat among the circle of easels. Laura loved the sunlight pouring in from the many skylights and creative energy. The group did more than paint, but it started with watercolors.

The subject of today's class rested in the center of the artists' circle—a series of colorful blocks piled into a large red bowl. The art instructor hushed all conversations and painting commenced. Laura relaxed into the process of creating and reinterpreting reality. Her brushes moved as if on their own, gliding across the canvas, transforming the emptiness to something more. Empowering her mind to nest in the beauty creating allotted.

The hum of her vibrating cellphone spooked her from her creative flow. She scooped it up and put her brush down. Quietly excusing herself, she went out into the hallway. She didn't recognize the number but perhaps one of the kids changed their number.

"Hello?"

Her cheerful greeting was met with heavy breathing.

"Hello?"

Labored breathing.

Laura rolled her eyes. She moved to hang up at the most-likely teenage caller.

"Don't you hang up on me, bitch." A distorted voice growled.

Laura froze, taken aback by the vulgar demand. Then with anger rolling forward, she said, "Don't contact me again."

She pressed the red phone icon, disconnecting the call. "Kids."

When she lowered the phone, she noticed her shaking hands. Once she returned to her seat, she gripped the chair's back. A wave of anxiety rolled over her for several long minutes. She called up her meditation training, taking deep breaths to calm her racing heart.

Deep breath. Hold. One, two, three. Release. Deep breath. Hold. One, two, three. Hold. Release.

As she regained her composure, she blocked the cell phone number.

"There."

A fragile peace settled over her.

"You feeling alright?" Maggie touched her shoulder. "You look a bit pale."

"Yeah, yeah, fine. Wrong number." Laura put her phone into her purse.

She tried to return to the flow, but the caller interrupted it. It was bizarre, a cruel joke, and it annoyed her as to why the caller contacted her.

I'm stressing and giving it too much power. Just some random butthead caller.

She shook it off. The strange caller faded into the background. Beneath her brushstrokes the red bowl and its contents transferred to canvas.

###

After painting class, Maggie and Hector strolled alongside Laura. The early spring day brought out the vibrant colors in gold and red the New Mexican flag and awnings. A variety of aromas surfed the breeze and rouse Laura's appetite. The air tasted delicious.

"…you'll see. They have hot fresh chiles and fry bread." Hector explained the menu options at Maria's Kitchen.

"Not too spicy. My stomach can't handle the hots anymore." Maggie adjusted her shoulder bag.

"They got salads." Hector smiled. "And posole."

"Oh good!" Maggie grinned.

Laura chuckled at their banter. Hector continued praising the new place.

A lurking black truck slithered into view. It followed them at a menacing pace, much to the frustration of surrounding traffic. Laura detached from her friends, half-listening to them. It drove by them slow with its windows blackened. She made out a male driver from the front windshield. It had lighter tint than the surrounding windows. They walked on through the sun-drenched day and after several blocks got to Maria's Kitchen.

In a blink of an eye, they were seated in a booth. Green chile and red chile salsas sat ready with a basket of tortilla chips for dipping. The server came over with three glasses of water. As she passed them out, she smiled, and said, "The usual, Hector?"

He nodded. "You know it, Bev."

Her dark eyes shifted to Maggie and Laura. "Do you need a menu?"

"Yes." Laura liked the restaurant's appearance. Although small, the tables had metal napkin holders painted with turquoise ovals and flowers. The front bank of windows overlooked the shopping area, the busy street, and pedestrians. They strolled about their day. Laura spied two little kids with what must be their parents, eating ice cream cones. The confection's melted creamy sugar raced down their small brown hands and arms.

The server returned with two laminated menus. "Here you go."

Laura took one of the menus and set about scanning the offerings. She wanted a frybread burger with green chile, and she prayed they had it. Just as she reached the sandwich section, a black smear caught her eye. She looked up with a knot in her stomach.

Is it the truck?

To her relief, the black sedan cruised past the window after a brief stop to allow pedestrians to cross. The crowd waved thanks and the car moved on. Feeling foolish, Laura sat upright and sighed.

"I'll have the grilled chicken salad with green chile," Maggie said, interrupting Laura's glare at the windows. "Ranch on the side."

"And for you, ma'am?" Bev held her hand out for Maggie's menu.

"The posole with a side of frybread." Laura's appetite had dwindled. If she didn't finish the meal, she could take it home to reheat for the following day.

The conversation turned to working with clay at the Artists' Studio tomorrow. Monday through Thursday, the studio offered classes for more mature people to engage their minds and their creativity. Tomorrow would be working with clay. Laura listened to Hector and Maggie talk about last week's class with mild interest. She skipped Wednesdays. Clay pushed her finger muscles and aching joints to their limits sometimes and she didn't feel connected to her creative stream.

In no time, Bev arrived with their orders. Hector's "usual" was a giant burrito, smothered in red and green chiles, sour cream and queso. He used a knife and fork to eat. In equal measure, Maggie's salad threatened to spill over its bowl. Her eye widened at the portion size. Laura's bowl of posole came last, but it didn't disappoint. The frybread took over its plate as to not be outdone.

Laura looked up at Bev. "I will need to-go containers."

Maggie raised her hand. "Me too."

Hector shook his head and kept eating.

Bev laughed. "Just about everyone does."

Laura smiled as she picked up the spoon and readied herself for lunch. Her shoulders relaxed, and it surprised her. She didn't realize she had tightened them. The first bite of posole sent tasty warmth through her body. Every muscle hummed in savory bliss, and the more she ate, the more she felt its heat envelope her like a glove.

Comfort food indeed.

Later, the trio walked back to the artist's studio and their parked vehicles. They said their goodbyes. As Laura pulled out of the lot in her Subaru Outback, she spied a black pickup truck with blackout windows.

There are scores of those trucks all over the pueblo.

She pushed the tingling worry to the back of her mind, but she switched lanes to get out of its way. Irate drivers were dangerous, and she liked to take her time driving home.

But it followed.

Humph. Laura drove on.

For another two miles, it trailed behind her, a black spot.

Am I really seeing this?

"Just go on!" Laura shouted to the driver, knowing he couldn't hear.

With adrenaline seeping in, she tightened her grip on the steering wheel. She wouldn't give in to road rage. The driver must've perceived some slight, so Laura slowed down and then made a right to try to lose him. Once she turned onto the parallel road, she sped through traffic. With frequent glances to her rearview mirror, she drove in circles until she stopped seeing black pickup trucks.

The long drive home settled her nerves. She parked her car in the garage and then walked outside to the front door to get the mail. The sound of her key in the door sent Chip into joyous barking. Laura put her Maria's Kitchen doggie bag on the island with the mail. She scooped up her dog and Chip licked her face in greeting.

"I missed you too." Laura laughed. "It's only been a few hours."

Laura held her for a few minutes more before placing her down on the floor.

"You act like you miss me. What you really want is this!" Laura took out the bag of dry dog food and shook it. Chip agreed.

She fed her dog, cleaned up the soiled puppy pads, and washed her hands. Laura took the mail from the counter and walked into her living room. She collapsed into her favorite chair and began sorting through the delivered items.

A flash of blue gave her pause.

Oh no. Please not another one.

With sweaty hands, she removed it from the others. A lump inched up her throat. The same elegant script addressed to her. Same address without a name or business. This time, it was bulky and firmer.

A card? As a grandma and mom, she'd received a fair number of cards in the mail.

She got up, claimed her letter opener, and sliced it.

Sure enough, a romantic card slid out. Decorated on the front were blue roses and gold script proclaiming love.

Huh? Is this a spurned or secret admirer?

But when she opened to the card's interior, she became sickened. An image depicting a man from the waist down, nude, slid out. It chilled her to the core.

What the hell? Why send me a photo?

Disgusted, she took the envelope, the photo, and the card over to the trash, and then thought to save it. She slipped the items into a plastic storage bag and shoved it in a drawer. Her phone buzzed from the depths of her purse. She fished it out and noticed a new text message. It had come earlier, but she hadn't heard it.

Her grandchildren didn't call. They texted. Few had time to engage anyone in legitimate conversation anymore. In her day, talking on the phone was a treat for teenagers. Now, no one could be bothered to write sentences. She chuckled. *Youth is wasted on the young.*

The text message read: I got your number.

Her knees weakened. Anxiety sprouted all over her. She rubbed her sweaty palms on her jeans.

He wants me to know it's him, again.

She deleted it and blocked the number. With speed, she rushed to the kitchen sink and washed her hands again. The looming filth lingered, so she lit some incense and sage to free her home of the negativity. She had no idea who he was, but she wanted his essence cleaned from her home. As she lowered the lights, and lit some candles, her energy and outlook improved. She checked the door locks and the windows before sinking onto her yoga mat in the living room.

After a deep breath, she clasped her hands together.

Ommmm.

Laura heard a loud *bang*. She bolted upright; a shriek lodged in her throat. With her heart hammering, she threw back the covers and quietly climbed out of bed. She inched down the short hallway and into the living room.

"Ha!" She crouched into a fighting stance, ready to tackle her attacker.

Instead, she found Chip, tail wagging in glee. She was also covered in dirt from the spilled cactus plant. Her tail tossed chunks of soil onto the floor.

"You gave me a heart attack." Laura laughed. "I'm too jumpy."

She went into the kitchen storage closet and took out the bare floors vacuum. As she dusted Chip off, the hushed quiet held a nervous tenor. Once done, Chip settled into her dog bed, now the excitement ended. She watched Laura with wide, round eyes.

"Don't get comfortable. You still need a bath." Laura warned as she started the vacuum.

Chip lowered her head onto her palms.

As Laura ran the device over tiny dirt mounds, the back of her neck tingled. She rubbed it with her free hand to soothe the gooseflesh. *Someone's watching me.* She spun around to her living room windows, nearly tripping over the cord. Outside, darkness cloaked all in night.

Is there some lunatic out there watching me?

With the chore done, Laura turned off the vacuum. She snatched the curtains closed. To end the nerves tingling, she checked the door's locks. The feeling retreated. She glanced at the clock, barely after 3 in the morning, the witching hour of the day. With her eyes burning, she walked around the home, checking the windows' locks. Living out in the rural sections of Taos didn't warrant locked doors. The biggest threats came from the winter weather and wildlife. Yet, the caller forced her to consider the biggest threats to her safety.

Once done with her security check, all traces of sleepiness retreated. She returned to her living room, this time with her hairbrush. After reigniting the fire, she sat in her chair and brushed her hair. She had to do something with her hands to calm herself down. Nearly to her waist, her gray streaked hair held less brown than it once did. Once she finished, she plaited it into one, thick braid. Chip slept on the dog bed in front of the fireplace, gnawing on a rawhide bone. Laura found comfort in routine. After several minutes, she settled into the cushions. The galloping of her heart lessened to a trot and then to its familiar rhythmic beating.

"You know what would make this better? Whiskey."

Laura got up and went over to the miniature bar to the left of the fireplace mantle. She took out a glass and bottle of *Scapa*. She then went to the refrigerator, removed a whiskey cube from the freezer and dropped it into the glass. Noting the time as a little after four, it was either too late to be drinking or too early.

Her phone rang. Its buzzing broke through the fire's crackle. A flash of anger tore through Laura and she reached into her robe, snatching it out of her pocket.

"What do you want?" Laura demanded.

"I'm looking for prey," the caller whispered.

His answer filled her with dread. Her skin crawled.

"What kind of prey?" *Let's try reason. Does he get logic?*

"Human." He snerked. "You."

"I'm no one's prey." Laura's knuckles ached from her grip on the phone.

"You already are…"

"Leave me alone!"

Click!

"Smug bastard!" Laura slammed the phone down so hard the case cracked against the kitchen island's counter. *Did I just pull the pin from the grenade?* She threw back her head and screamed as loud and for long as she could.

Chip barked awake, startled by her outburst. She raced over to check on her owner. She whimpered in worry.

"Now, whiskey." Laura glanced down at Chip. "And none for you."

The whiskey's burning warmth eased Laura into a rough slumber around seven just as dawn turned the New Mexican dawn a watery pink. As soon as she shut her eyes and fell into sleep's arms, the crunch of tires on gravel and the motorized hum of an idling made woke her. She froze. A sinking feeling plunged her deeper beneath the covers. The buzzing went on forever. After tossing and turning, she threw back her covers, heart pounding.

Is it him? Has he finally come to claim his prey?

She sipped a breath.

You are Laura Snow. What would Abraham think of you cowering under the covers? Get up. Protect what's yours. No one is gonna do it for you. You don't cower to fear.

With her inner coach on drill sergeant mode, Laura climbed out of bed. Still dressed in her robe and trembling, she inched down the hallway toward the front of the house to the guest room. Once she reached the blinds, she parted them and peaked out. The mail carrier pushed items into the mailbox with a huge heap of boredom. She wore a hat and sunglasses along with the U.S. Postal Service uniform. She lumbered back into her pickup, a battered old white and blue Ford, and drove off.

The level of aggravation hit Laura like a ton of bricks.

The mail carrier! I'm jumping at the mail, now.

But Laura's brief relief became cold anxiety. *Is there another letter in there?*

She left the guest bedroom. She decided the mail could wait.

The clock gave the time as a bit after eleven. So, Laura decided to make some tea. All hope of restful slumber evaporated, and she padded around the kitchen, getting her favorite teacup and loose-leaf tea. Today required something strong, so a black tea blend. Hearing the stirring in the kitchen, Chip came in to see about breakfast.

"Why is this guy bothering me?" Laura asked her.

Chip barked at the back door.

"Right, morning walkies," Laura said.

She changed into jogging pants and sweatshirt and sandals. Once she grabbed the lease, Chip barked and ran in circles in excitement. Laura looked at the cell phone. She didn't want to be out of the house without it in case something happened. The rural terrain around her home came with potential hazards. So, with her heart pounding, she turned the power back on.

26 missed calls. Dozens of what must be angry text messages waited to be read.

The phone beeped.

She opened the door and its screen, refusing to pay any attention to the notifications. They walked and once she reached the clearing, she took Chip off the lease. She bound forward into the yard, barking at birds, and chasing prairie dogs. Once they reached the pond, Laura's phone rang.

She let it go to voicemail, knowing it was full. While she absorbed the vitamin D, she decided to check the messages. She didn't want to miss anything important from her grandchildren or from Hector or Maggie.

The first text message from an unknown number:

```
I'm gonna stalk that ass.
```

Laura's fingers hit the correct keystrokes by habit. *Delete. Block.*

She glanced at the voicemail number. It came from an entirely different phone number. Her finger wavered a moment above the latest message. She licked her dry lips and pressed play. Her hands damp with anticipation as the familiar voice spoke.

"I'm watching you." His voice had an edge unlike before.

It made Laura shudder.

Click. Block. Delete.

"Chip! Chip! Come on. Let's go in!" Laura hugged herself, Chip's lease clasped in her hand. "Let's go eat."

At the mention of food, the dusty Pomeranian trotted over to Laura, and together they went back across the yard and into the house.

Once Laura hung up the lease, Chip went over to her empty food bowl.

"I refuse to sit here and be a victim. I'm going to go get my number changed today. That should stop him." Laura declared.

She bent down to Chip's dry food container, opened it, and scooped some kibble into her bowl. These habitual actions occurred almost with her notice. Her mind focused on her caller. It had become painfully clear the person who sent the letter, the photo, the text messages, and the phone calls were all the same.

"He's right. I *am* being stalked."

The acknowledgment hit her like a ton of bricks. Stalking didn't happen to women her age. It happened to college students and pretty young things who rejected boyfriends or men too immature and narcissistic to accept the woman's decision.

Not to 57 years old divorced women.

At the thought of him, her phone buzzed. She could hear it from the bedroom where she'd left it on the nightstand. It was surreal. As soon as one call ended, another one began, bleeding into an endless stream of anxiety.

My demand for him to stop fell on deaf ears.

She marched into her bedroom, snatched up the device, and powered it off.

The heavy silence hung in the room. She closed her eyes and tried to push back against the fatigue threatening to overtake her. Each creak and coyote howl startled her. She retreated to the bright and sunny kitchen, and to her tea kettle's cry with annoyance strumming her nerves.

She poured the steaming water into her teacup, steeped her leaves for the required minutes and sat down at her kitchen table.

"I don't know what he'll do next," Laura confessed to Chip. "But I know what I'm doing today. I'm not going to clay work class, but over to the cell phone store to switch out my number."

She took a quick sip of her tea.

In the background, his calls and messages came like water torture, *drip, drip, drip.*

Laura realized she was drowning.

After getting her phone number changed, an exhausted and embarrassed, Laura approached her front door, having parked her vehicle outside the garage. She didn't get the mail but followed the footpath to her flat two steps and up to the semi-round porch. At once she noticed the door's screen.

"My word. What?"

It had been slashed, and it bore gaping punctured holes. The rest of the screen bore nails. Fear gripped her heart. She swallowed the acidic taste of adrenaline and scurried around to the side of the house where her bedroom faced the road leading up to her home. There she discovered footprints in the dirt beneath her window.

Her stomach dropped. *He's been here. He actually come here!*

Her stalker had her address but to come to her home took the threat from being distant and annoying to downright frightening. The threat had marched right up to her sanctuary and violated it. He didn't just slash away her screen, but her sense of safety, too.

Wild barking roused Laura from her panic attack. Chip remained inside. She debated whether to go in. What if her attacker had broken in? What if he held Chip hostage? She didn't see any signs of a break in, but what if she missed something. What if Chip's barking was a warning to her? Not wanting to run into her assailant, she retreated to her Subaru and locked all the doors.

She called the police.

"911, what's your emergency?"

"Someone's broken into my home." Laura realized she was whispering and cleared her throat. "Please send the police."

"Someone broke into your home?" The 911 operator parroted back.

"Yes, please, come quick." Laura's hands trembled.

"What's your address ma'am?"

Laura gave it to her.

"Get to someplace safe. The police are on their way. Stay on the line with me, ma'am."

"Okay. I'm in my car."

As she waited for Tao's finest, her stalker had no sense of personal boundaries. She gripped the steering wheel to keep her free hand from shaking. *Goddess, what did I do to deserve this?*

It felt like hours until the police cruiser arrived. It didn't have on its lights, but it pulled silently alongside her parked car in the drive, blocking her in.

"The police are here." Laura reported to the operator.

"Great. You can hang up now."

A thin, young police officer approached her car, while another one exited the passenger side of the cruiser and headed toward the house. The one outside her door had dark, nearly black hair and a thick moustache. "Ma'am. Roll down your window."

Instead, Laura got out of the vehicle. "Someone's broke in…"

"Good afternoon ma'am. I'm Officer Martinez. Are you all right?"

"Yes, I came home and found my front door…" She couldn't finish, so she gestured at the damaged screen and her porch.

"Did you go into the house?"

"No, but my dog is inside, barking, her head off."

"Okay. Get back in the car. We'll take a look around."

Laura did as instructed, locking the doors as she did so. She couldn't believe he'd come to her house. She tried to follow the two officers as they rounded the house and then circled back to the front again. She lost sight of them, but a few minutes later, Officer Martinez came over to her again.

"We don't see any signs of forced entry and all of the windows appeared to be locked as well as the doors. Do you have the key to the front? We'll do a sweep inside of the house for you."

With her heart hammering like a blacksmith's forge, she passed her keys to the police officer, noting the one for the front door. She grabbed her purse and climbed out of the vehicle.

"You see what he's done to the screen?" Laura gestured to the damage.

Officer Martinez said, "Yes, ma'am. We have taken pictures of the vandalism."

"Vandalism? He tried to break in!"

"There's no evidence of an attempt to get inside the home." Officer Martinez unlocked the door and the other officer gently guided Laura back as he followed. "Stay here."

The patting of small feet and nails on tiles came rushing toward them. Chip growled at the police officers and commenced barking. It wasn't her usual bark, but something deeper, closer to warning, than a cheerful greeting.

They ignored her and continued on into the home. Laura remained on the porch.

"Come here." She reached out for Chip.

The petite puppy growled again, low, and deep, but decided she missed Laura more than giving the officers a strong talking to. She trotted over to her owner and allowed Laura to sweep her up into a hug, which she sorely needed.

"Thank you, my little protector." She kissed Chip's head.

The officers disappeared into the house. Every few moments, one of them would pop out into the hallway, gun drawn, shouting, "Taos Police Department!"

Time went by like molasses, when finally, both officers returned to the front porch. Officer Martinez reholstered his gun and came up to her.

His partner, an athletic woman with dark brown hair wrapped in a bun, and hazel eyes stood behind him. Her arms akimbo, her sunglasses rested on her head.

"No one is there and there aren't signs of a break in. It does look like you have some vandalism done to the front screen door. We can investigate it, but I'll be honest with you. It's probably some teenagers screwing around." Officer Martinez shrugged.

"Listen, I know who did this and it isn't a teenager." Laura petted Chip who growled in confirmation.

"You do?" Officer Martinez's eyes widened. He took out his notebook and pencil from his front pocket. "If you have a suspect, tell me."

"Well, I don't know his name..." Laura started.

"How do you know who it is?" Officer Martinez's face fell, and his shoulders slumped.

"I'm being stalked." Laura's cheeks warmed and her hands dampened with cold sweat. "He's been calling, text messaging, and sending items in the mail."

"Do you have any idea what he looks like?"

"No, I don't." Laura didn't like his tone.

"How do you know it's the same person texting and calling?" Officer Martinez put his materials away.

"Why are you interrogating me? This person has escalated, clearly. He's come to my house and attacked." Laura's heartbeat sped up. It pounded against her chest. Her entire face was aflame. No doubt she was as red as a beet.

"I'm sorry ma'am. We'll file a report and see if we can find out who vandalized your door. There's no evidence he's done anything illegal or this person's identity. It's difficult for us to get involved."

"Stalking *is* illegal!" Laura handed him her cellphone. "Look for yourself. There's footprints beneath my window and he destroyed my screen door."

"We can't prove conclusively that it's *any* suspect or person, but it's harmless prank calls, most likely..."

"I'm a prisoner in my own home. He follows me around..." Laura's words fumbled over each other as her fear wretched up. If the police won't help her, then she was truly on her own. "A black pickup truck…"

"Have you tried changing your phone number?" Officer Martinez asked as he took her phone. He swiped and pushed buttons, reviewing the messages.

This cannot be real. After everything he's done. No one takes it seriously.

"These are from different phone numbers." Officer Martinez glanced up from her device.

"Yes, but if you listen to the voicemail messages, they all have the same voice." Laura countered, her frustration making her voice whiny. "Surely, there's something you can do."

Officer Martinez returned her phone and met her frustrated glare. "Keep a log. Document the encounters. Install cameras. We'll be in touch."

He didn't wait for a reply. As Laura watched his back as he marched off toward his cruiser, she wanted to cry. She released an annoyed grunt and turned to go inside when the other officer stepped forward.

"Ma'am. I'm Officer Gomez. You're right. Stalking is a crime, and what this person is doing to you, is against the law. Here's the card of Detective Perez. He handles cases like yours. Give him a call and do what Officer Martinez said. Keep a log. Document. So, when we do catch this guy, you have evidence to put him away."

Laura took it. "Thank you."

Officer Gomez nodded. "Your home is safe. We swept every closet, the garage, and each room. Go inside, lock up, and keep your phone charged. Oh, and call Detective Perez in the morning."

"I will." Laura removed the keys from the lock and shut the door behind her. Officer Gomez waited until Laura locked and bolted the door before stepping off the porch and returning to the cruiser, idling behind the Subaru.

Laura put Chip down once they got inside and dropped Detective Perez's card on the island. Barely four in the afternoon, and Laura already wanted to shower and go to bed. But first, she went to her bedroom closet and removed the black box from the top shelf. She returned to the kitchen table.

Petrified something would happen, Laura took out her gun and its cleaning kit. No matter what she did, her stalker managed to stay a step ahead and right in step with the rules. If the police couldn't help protect her, then it fell to her.

She had to be ready. "We need to take precautions, Chip."

Her fluffy dog retreated to her dog bed and looked on wearily. She didn't like the noise guns made.

Thursday

Laura's gut instinct woke her. Chip roused from her bed with nose nudges. On the end table beside her, the gun, a .38, remained on the table next to the empty whiskey glass. She fell asleep in the living room, unable to get comfortable in the bed. A nagging feeling pushed her to her feet. She shuffled to the front door and she looked out the window. In the early morning light, she discovered a box on her porch.

The U.S. Postal Service delivered through all kinds of weather, but they didn't drop off boxes at 7 am in the morning. She went out to the porch. The box had no postage and no return address.

She walked back into the kitchen, scooped up the card and called Detective Perez. If she called 911, she'd get some idiot like Martinez. No, she wouldn't fool around anymore. They'd only mock her.

"Do you know what time it is?" The detective asked in lieu of a greeting.

"Officer Gomez said you'd help me. My name is Laura Snow. The stalker left something on my porch. I dunno if it's a bomb, or a weapon of some kind…" Saying it aloud made it sound creepier and crazier.

"Slow down. Ma'am! Slow down." Laura heard some rustling, some whispers, and then the detective returned to the phone. "What's your name again?"

"Laura Snow."

"Ms. Snow, why didn't you call 911?"

"I, I didn't want to get someone else who wouldn't listen to me or who would be dismissive," Laura explained. "This man vandalized my door yesterday and now he's put a package on my porch." She swallowed the quiver in her voice and the rush of hot tears.

"Okay, ma'am. Don't touch it. Give me your address. I'll be right there." Detective Perez sounded confident and awake.

"Oh, I won't touch the ting."

"Be right there."

Detective Perez and two police officers arrived at Laura's house half an hour later. She'd showered and put on decent clothes, fed Chip and let her out for a little run. Lacking an appetite, Laura had brewed a cup of white tea with honey to calm her nerves. She watched the detective climb out of the unmarked police car and meet with the other two officers. They put on latex gloves and approached the house. One of the police officers had a camera, and the other one had some device Laura didn't recognize.

While the other two officers evaluated the plain box on the porch, Detective Perez knocked on her door. He wore a straw cowboy hat and had shoulder-length hair. They bore gray streaks, and he was clean shaven. He had earrings in both ears and a necklace around his neck. Unlike the other police officers, Perez didn't wear a uniform, but a blue jean button down shirt and jeans. Silver bracelets decorated his wrists.

"Ms. Snow. It's Detective Perez." He knocked. "I'm here about the box."

Chip bolted to the door, barking furiously at the stranger's intrusion.

Laura scooped Chip up and unlocked the door. "Detective."

"Ma'am. May I come in?"

"Yes, please." Laura stepped back, allowing him room to enter. He stood tall, definitely above six feet, not counting the hat. He removed it once inside and shut the door behind.

"Can I get you anything?" Laura asked.

"No ma'am. Is there some place we can talk?"

"Sure, this way." Laura placed Chip down, but she growled at the act.

"Who's this?" Perez squatted down to Chip. He removed one of his latex gloves and held out his hand for her to sniff.

"Chipotle, Chip for short." Laura smiled as Chip bared her teeth.

"It's nice to meet you both." Perez stood back up, replacing the glove. "Though I wish it was under different circumstances."

Laura led him into the living room, where she threw a blanket over the gun before sitting down in her chair. She gestured for the detective to sit on the sofa, which he did. The sofa sat across from the fireplace, mini bar, and Laura's favorite chair.

He sat on the cushion's edge. "On the way over, I read Officer Martinez's report about the vandalism to your front porch. The CSI techs outside will be dusting it for prints and removing it as evidence. You may want to get someone to replace it today, if you can."

"Thank you." Laura breathed a little easier.

"I did talk to Officer Gomez, who, in full disclosure, is my niece. Any reason why someone is harassing you?"

"Do I need one?" Laura crossed her arms.

"No, ma'am." Perez kept a sober expression. "Sometimes, if there's a connection, a breakup, a squabble, a fight, or something that sparks the stalker's anger or fixation, it helps us track down who's doing it. It gives us a suspect and a place to start. But anyone can be a victim."

"I don't know who's doing this, but it started with a letter."

"You still have the letter?"

Laura got up and went to the kitchen where she retrieved the plastic bag. She returned with it and she passed it to Perez.

"I don't have the first one, but I did keep the second one." Laura sat back down.

Perez, still wearing gloves, took the items out of the bag, one at a time. He read the card. Then he looked at the photo. His face never changed. It remained a stoic blank surface.

"I'll turn this over to the lab as well." Perez put items back into the plastic bag and placed it beside his hat on the sofa. "Start at the beginning and tell me everything that's happened."

Laura hesitated. "This feels so foolish. I changed my phone number and…"

"You're not alone, Ms. Snow. Over three million people are stalked in the U.S. each year. They don't quit. Some people don't survive these encounters…"

She looked him dead in the eye. "I will."

"Good. Help me catch him. Tell me everything."

She did and when she finished, she passed her phone over to him. Perez took it and began scrolling. He sat quiet with only his purple latex fingers moving over the device.

Minutes ticked by. With her phone in the detective's hand, she felt naked and exposed. Like most people, a big chunk of her life existed on her device, and having a stranger going through it made her feel like he raffled through her clothes while she wore them.

With a flourish, Perez handed her phone back. "He's escalating and he's becoming more dangerous. Did you call a locksmith?"

"No, why?"

"For the door." Perez jutted his head toward the front door. "I would get the locksmith to change the locks."

"Was anything missing?"

"My sense of safety." Laura rubbed her arms to remove the goosebumps. "The officers said he didn't gain entry."

Perez sighed. "I'm sorry this is happening to you, Ms. Snow."

"Laura."

"Ma'am?"

"Call me Laura." Laura figured she'd better get to know the detective since they'd be in contact through the ordeal. "There doesn't appear to be any stopping him." Laura rubbed her burning, fatigued eyes. "I'm so tired. The constant stress is emotionally taxing. Every noise sets my nerves on edge."

Now she had an audience that listened, all of her pent-up emotions poured out. Perez sat still, allowing her frustrations and fears to roll over him. Nothing in him stirred. He didn't take notes, he didn't demean her or tell her she should be grateful someone paid attention to her. He only affirmed what she knew in her gut with a head nod. He sat with his hands tented in front of him.

The threat was real, and it had to be stopped.

"Sir, you'll want to come see this?" An officer came into the living room. She had short brunette hair and a stocky build. She nodded in greeting at Laura and then headed back down the hallway and out the front door. The screen *whapped* as it closed.

"Excuse me, Ms. Snow." Perez put his hat on and picked up the plastic bag.

Laura got up too and followed him to the porch. Perez exited the house, but she stayed behind the tortured screen door, watching. She didn't think it was a bomb because the officers had opened it and one sat seated beside it. Unlocked forensic kits sat opened on the ground around the box, and Perez stood with his arms crossed just to the right of the door.

"What's in the box?" he asked.

Laura peered through her door as one of the CSI Techs lifted a dog squeaker toy. It had been bagged already.

"Gifts for a dog. Does she have a dog?" The tech put that one back and lifted another item.

"Chip. Oh goddess, he knows about my dog." Laura groaned. "He's been watching me. This is proof."

"It's a box of toys, sir," the other tech said.

"The suspect trespassed on this property. Fingerprint the box. I want all of it sent to the lab." Perez bent down. "There's no mailing address or postage. That means he brought it here."

Laura's throat closed over the scream pulsating in her throat. That's two straight days he'd come directly up to her property. Perez confirmed it.

Funny, she hadn't received any calls or text messages today.

It's early yet.

Perez turned back to her and came inside again, removing his hat. "Ms. Snow, we're going to take the box, the card, and other items with us to the station to see if we can get some forensics off of these items. You have my number if anything else happens."

"That's it?" Laura put her hands in her pockets to keep them from shaking.

"Is there someone you can stay with or who can come stay with you until this is all over?"

Laura thought of the children, all grown and living their lives. She couldn't burden them with her little problem. Not to mention, she had no idea where Abraham was, and she didn't want to endanger Samantha and the kids.

"No, I don't." Laura met Perez's somber gaze.

Perez nodded as if he understood. "When you're home, keep this place locked up tight. If you go out, try to stay in large groups or with people you know. You don't know who this person is, but they know you. So be careful and observant."

"I will."

"You got a conceal and carry permit for that gun?" Perez asked, the first hints of a grin tugged at his full lips.

"Yes, I do." Laura's cheeks warmed at being caught.

"Good. Use it. I'll be in touch."

With that, he turned on his booted heel and left.

Friday

"You okay? You don't seem like yourself." Maggie touched Laura's shoulder, making her jump. "Sorry. Didn't mean to startle you."

Laura gave her a thin smile. "It's these phone calls and text messages. It's driving me nuts. I can't sleep."

Maggie paused mid brushstroke. "You can block those telemarketers, pesty bastards. Jose told me there's an app you can download to automatically block them. Apparently, there's an app for everything now."

"Thanks for the tip." A flush of shame kept her from saying more. Laura swept her paint brush upward. Green oil covered across the blank canvas, setting the background of verdant mountains. With her free hand, she touched her crystal and forced a grin to Maggie. "Your mountains look alive there…"

Maggie laughed. "I do love hiking you know."

In the cool sliver of the day, a realization dawned on Laura. She couldn't sit at home, waiting for something to happen. She'd spent the rest of Thursday locked up tight in her home, but today, she ventured out. After the long, cold winter, she longed for spring and sun. So, she'd come down to the Artist's Studio for Free-for-All Friday. She'd chosen painting, and Hector and Maggie joined her.

Hector, seated on the other side of Laura, leaned over. "Who's bothering you?"

"I wish I knew, but the boogie man has no face." Laura met Hector's questioning eyes.

"You dunno."

"No. It's probably some kid getting his kicks. I'm too old for crank calls."

Hector scowled, his thick eyebrows forming a fat, hairy caterpillar. "This sounds like a little more than harmless prank calls."

A rush of heat raced up Laura's neck. She avoided direct eye contact and continued painting. "It's fine. You know, I chart my own course. Now, are we going back to that restaurant today? The one with the good sopapillas."

Despite changing her number, the mysterious phone calls from a predator inched up frequency. She didn't know how he got her new number, but her bliss lasted only one day. The calls numbered in double digits every day. The constant texting, calls, and hang-ups drained her, but moreover, talking about it out loud, to human beings, not dogs, made it all sound foolish. Even the police, except the detective.

Hector started to speak, hesitated, and then said, "You mean, Maria's? Great food."

Thankful both of her friends hadn't pressed, Laura tried to relax into her creative work. She pushed the stalker from her mind, invoking her mindfulness of being present in the moment. As her hand maneuvered the paintbrush, her shoulders relaxed, and her stress lessened. Each stroke swept the anxiety away. Soon, she lost herself in the painting, disappearing into the colors and details, the unfolding and birth of an image, a place, a moment, a feeling made visible.

She hadn't heard from Perez, but she didn't really expect to get any updates so soon. Real life took time. Hector took the hint and stopped questioning her.

Before long, the session ended. The trio along with others from class washed their brushes, dried them, and put up their easels. Hector and Maggie appeared restless as they collected their belongings. As they left the studio, Hector spoke first.

"You should take those phone calls seriously. You can go to the police."

Laura nodded. "Yeah."

"Have you already talked to them?" Maggie pipped up from the right side of Laura.

"Yes."

Hector shrugged. "Good. Now they got a record of it in case, you know, it becomes more than you think."

They made a right out of the studio and headed down the two blocks to Maria's Kitchen. Another gorgeous afternoon glistened overhead. She rubbed dry paint off her knuckles when a dark object glided alongside them and pulled into an empty space. A black truck idled along the street. It looked familiar with its dark tinted windows, but black pickup trucks were a dime a dozen in Taos.

Once they walked by, it pulled out of its parking space and followed them in a slow crawl.

Laura's phone rang. She broke out in a cold sweat. Neither Hector or Maggie seemed to notice.

Hector head it. "Don't answer it."

Maggie took Laura's right arm and wrapped it in hers. "Look Maria's is right there. I can already smell the goodies. Do you?"

She didn't answer, but no sooner had it gone to voicemail, did her phone buzz again. It happened over and over again so that by the time they reached the restaurant, Laura snatched the phone out of her purse, pressed the green voice icon and uttered, "Leave me alone!

The voice slithered out in response. "Calm down. It's Friday!"

Her blood ran cold. "Stop calling me."

"You're gonna pay for yelling at me bitch." Heavy breathing.

Click.

Maggie glanced over to Hector and then to Laura. "Come on. Let's get you some good food. That'll settle you."

This cannot be my life.

Once inside Maria's Kitchen, Bev got them seated and they ordered sans menus.

"I need this nightmare to be over." Laura ran her hands through her hair. Her shoulders ached in concert with her neck pain. She rubbed her muscles.

"You're clearly not sleeping." Maggie sipped her ice water with lemon. "Those bags can carry out a week's worth of groceries."

Laura turned her silver ring around as Maggie continued.

"You should get a massage! There's a great spa down on Tate Street."

Laura agreed. "You're right. It can help realign my chakras."

"Good for stress too. Let them work out those toxins." Maggie elbowed her and winked.

Laura closed her eyes. She wanted sleep but napping in the chair barely came close to restful slumber. "What's the name of the place?"

"Taos Spa."

"Tourist trap." Laura opened her eyes. The name invoked coral and turquoise paint and fake, glued Kachinas.

Maggie laughed. "Yes, but quality massages. Promise."

Bev brought their food, and they dug in. It smelled like savory heaven and now that she'd relaxed a little, Laura bit into her chicken and green chile burrito chunk. She decided to try Hector's favorite, the Maria Burrito, and it didn't disappoint. Swimming with cheese and green chile, the meal required a fork and a spoon.

Her phone buzzed. She checked it almost without thinking. The message contained no words, but a picture—of her!

Wearing the same pink blouse and khaki pants she had on now. Eating the same burrito.

Laura swallowed. *He's here!*

She scanned the crowded restaurant. Cell phones existed everywhere. It could be anyone. Not only did he come to her house, but he'd followed her here.

She didn't want to let on he upset her. Uneasy, Laura forced a smile at Maggie beside her.

"This is delicious." Laura pointed with her fork.

Maggie nodded in agreement. She'd ordered the grilled chicken salad. Again.

"You know," Hector said, grabbing her attention, "I can come over tonight. Look around. So, you're not alone."

"Don't worry. I can handle it." Shivers of fear blanketed her even as she spoke those words, knowing her stalker sat among the patrons. Her apprehension made her hesitate.

"I'm not gonna hurt you." Hector put down his fork.

Detective Perez's words came back to her. She shouldn't be alone in the house.

"Sure, Hector. That'll be fine." Laura gave in. Perez suggested the same thing.

"I'll order pizza." Hector nodded, his moustache twitching.

Laura leaned over her burrito and whispered to him "It's not a date. I feel I have to say that."

"Of course not. I'm doing my friend a favor." Hector scowled as if offended.

Maggie snorted into her salad.

Later, when Laura walked into her home, a hot and humid fist punched her for a loop. Chip panted at the door. She put her groceries on the island and walked over to check the thermostat.

It had been changed to heat. Laura frowned.

"I know I didn't have a senior moment and changed it."

She switched it back to cool, but the feeling of safety dissolved again. As she recounted her steps from this morning, her phone buzzed. She rechecked the lock on her door and the garage door too. Both locked up tight.

After giving Chip water with ice in her bowl, she said, "I guess I did change it. Not sleeping must be doing a number on my noggin."

Chip lapped up her water. Laura opened her phone and noted the new message notification. The text read:

`Your real hot`

Laura's heart inched into her throat at the confirmation and poor grammar. "He's been in the house!"

An hour later, Detective Perez arrived with two more police officers around six. Laura stood by the kitchen island as the techs walked through her home, checking for signs of a break in. Beside her, Perez read the text message, wrote down the information in a notepad. He handed the device back to her.

"Here, I want you to make a statement. Start from the time you got home until you called me." Perez passed her a sheet of paper and a pen. "Tell me everything. Don't leave anything out."

The techs fanned out everywhere and Chip barked at them all. She raced around them, in joy, pretending to be upset at the intrusion. She hadn't seen this many people inside the house since Samantha visited with the kids.

Perez stood beside Laura. His arms were crossed over his chest, but his cowboy hat rested against his torso.

"You didn't know him or invite him to call you. Did you?"

"No. Everything about him rubs me the wrong way." Laura couldn't believe he'd even asked the question.

"There's something brewing underneath. He's escalating." Perez spoke more to himself than to her.

Laura rubbed her hands on her pants. "I'm afraid he might take more drastic action. He has this unbridled rage toward me."

"It does look like he's rapidly descending into madness."

"I don't wanna see him unhinged." Chills skated down Laura's back.

At that moment, a police officer walked up. He said, "Sir, we discovered some discarded cigarettes butts and apple cores around the rear of the house."

Perez glanced at her. "Do you smoke?"

"No."

He looked back to the officer. "Get it to the lab. Let's check for DNA."

The officer nodded and left. Perez turned to look at Laura.

"Look. This guy's driven by rage. He's addicted to the high he gets from tormenting you. He's been hanging out here. You should go somewhere else."

Laura shook her head. "I'm not leaving my home."

"You are stubborn. You know that? Is this building worth your life?" The hint of annoyance made his words bite.

"No, of course it isn't." Laura shot back. She couldn't explain why she didn't want to run away from the stalker. If she started now, she'd never stop running, always looking over her shoulder. This needed to end.

The sooner. The better.

"I'm tired of this. Aren't you?" She looked down at Chip.

She barked in affirmation.

Friday evening

Hector picked up a pair of latex gloves from the living room's end table. "These yours. Don't seem like your style."

"No but they belong to someone." With a weak laugh, Laura grabbed a plastic storage bag and used her fingertips put them inside. She sealed it and placed them on the counter. She'd ask Perez later.

"Detective Perez leave those behind?" He shook his head. "He ain't done too much so far."

Laura couldn't argue with that, so she didn't.

A few knocks rasped against the door.

"Pizza's here." Hector headed to the front door. The pistol sat in the small of his back.

Laura followed him and stood in the hall while Hector approached the door. He put his hand to the curtain before looking outside. She held her breath.

"Yeah, it's the pizza guy." Hector opened the door and pushed the screen open a crack. He exchanged money for the warm cardboard box of goodies.

Laura liked having someone here. She hated to admit it, but the fact the person was a man helped. Some men only respected other males. She smiled at Hector's back. Perez had been right. She *did* need someone here with her. As Hector moved away from the door, she spied the pizza driver's vehicle in the front—a black truck. A chill spilled over her, but heat rose from her toes to her face.

Fury.

Before she thought about it, she pushed past Hector, out onto the porch, and down the path to the vehicle.

"Ma'am?" The pizza delivery driver paused with his red-hot tote crammed beneath his arm.

This can't be him. Can it?

Laura stopped short. The voice, *his* voice, came with confusion. It didn't have the sinister confidence of her predator stalker.

"Did you need something?" The driver put one foot inside his truck. "I got, uh, other deliveries."

"No, I wanted to see if you got your tip." Laura's voice shook, and she swallowed the acidic spit in her mouth.

"Thanks, but he tipped already." The slice of annoyance raised his tone an octave. "Goodnight."

Embarrassment made her face burn. With a tense sigh, she fell back as he slammed the driver's side door and drove off.

But not before Laura memorized the license plate.

She went inside, locked the door, and went to the island. Once she pulled out the pad and pen, she scribbled down the license plate. Beside her, Hector had opened the pizza box and placed two slices of pepperoni and cheese on a paper plate. He slid it over to Laura. Then he repeated it for himself.

"What's your plan?" Hector bit into his folded slice. Cheese oozed out of the bottom and dropped to his plate.

"Never answer my phone again." Laura found New York style pizza in northern New Mexico strange. She bit into her slice and chewed the hot cheese and crust. "I already changed my phone number."

"Pain in the ass. You shouldn't have to do that." Hector's empty plate spoke to his hunger.

"Do you just inhale your food?" Laura laughed.

She had a slice and a half left, plus the other half of the pizza. A bottle of antacids rested alongside cans of diet soda.

"Cops, number change, and the jerk's still at it. I'm getting 40 to 50 calls a day."

"Why don't you turn it off?"

"I do, sometimes. When I turn it back on my voice mail is full of his vile garbage. My text messages number in the hundreds." Laura took another bite and chewed. She didn't feel like eating, but she kept at it for Hector.

Hector whistled. "Damn."

"You can say that again."

Hector grinned. "I'm sorry, Laura. You don't deserve this."

"No one does."

Hector popped open a can of soda. "We'll find a way to stop him."

Although she didn't believe him, it was a nice thought.

###

For a couple of weeks, the phone calls and text messages stopped. Her phone stopped vomiting up threats and harassment. Life returned to its normal calm mornings and afternoon walks with Chip. Lunch on Tuesdays and Thursdays with the Taos crew, and Wednesday clean house day. She almost let her guard down. Perhaps breaking into her home had been the peak of her stalker escalation.

On Monday, Laura left the organic grocery store with a bag of fresh vegetables for tonight's dinner. Her phone rang and without thinking, she answered.

"Hello." She sounded breathless, and she rebuked herself for not waiting until she got into the car.

"You really shouldn't be out alone." His voice hadn't changed in the weeks since she last heard it.

Laura froze as her heart sank. She slumped against her vehicle. "Stop calling me."

"Oh, no. This isn't going to end. That's for sure." He laughed and hung up.

With her hands shaking, she climbed into her vehicle and drove toward her home, but as she got to the next block from the grocery store, the black truck glided into view. Two cars behind her, the blacked-out front window loomed above the others.

Who the hell are you?

Her heart started to race as she switched lanes, made a left on a red light, trying to leave him behind. It shot forward, but the two cars blocked its path. Relief washed over her, and made an immediate right, trying to get home before he could catch up. She didn't know why she bothered.

He *knew* where she lived.

But his creeping behind her, stalking her with that troubling truck made her heart drop into her stomach. Her phone rang, and she answered with "Leave me alone!"

"You think you got away. I will be coming over there, one way or another." With the unspoken thread lodged in her heart, the caller hung up.

The rest of the way home she didn't see him again.

That didn't make her feel any better.

Half an hour later, Detective Perez stood in the center of Laura's living room, reading the text messages on her phone. One hand held his cowboy hat against his thigh, and the other scrolled through messages. Her groceries sat on the island, still in their plastic bags.

"Did you find fingerprints or DNA from the break in?" Laura stroked Chip, who she held cradled in her arms. She sat in her chair with her ankles crossed and her heart pounding.

Perez looked up from the phone. "We haven't gotten the DNA back. The crime scene techs only found smudges on the thermostat and no fingerprints on the windows. He probably wore gloves."

"Why is he calling again? He left me alone for weeks and now, he's started all over again. He's threatening me."

Perez nodded. "I know. Something's provoked him. It has nothing to do with you. You're just a focal point of his anger."

"Why? I don't even know who it is."

Chip whimpered and Laura realized she held her too tight. She loosened her grip on her dog.

Perez shook his head. "I can't explain why they fixate on certain people, but it is most likely someone you met or showed some kindness or attention."

Laura shook her head. "That doesn't make any sense. He's repaying my kindness with threats, violence, and harassment?"

Perez handed her phone back to her. "I'm not saying I understand it. Just that it's the way it is."

"I need to understand." Laura shouted.

Chip barked and struggled to get out of her arms. She put the wiggling dog down.

"I'm sorry. I shouldn't have shouted." Laura rubbed her hands on her pants. "I'm tired."

"Let's go for coffee." Perez put his cowboy hat back on. "You can't sit here like a prisoner."

It wasn't dark when Detective Perez dropped Laura off at home. He didn't wait in the unmarked car to watch her go in but climbed out of the vehicle to escort her up to the house. Once she unlocked the door, he went inside of the home, sweeping each room, closet, and the garage with his weapon out, and his cowboy hat on. Laura remained by the front door, with a relieved Chip at her feet. Laura's hands clenched into fists at the possibility Perez would encounter her stalker. Her throat closed over the knot of growing fear. She couldn't swallow it due to her dry mouth.

I just need this to be over. I can't have a detective every day and night checking my home.

Detective Perez reappeared from the garage. "All clear. No one lurking, but Imma look around outside too. You lock up after me. Okay?"

Laura nodded as the tight bind of anxiety loosened a little.

"You got your phone on you? Your gun is where?"

Laura took the phone from her back jean pocket and showed it to him. "It's on the nightstand."

Detective Perez came up to her and clasped her on the shoulder. "Listen, if you hear anything. Call 911. If you can, call me afterwards."

"Okay."

He pointed at Chip. "You look out for her. Got it? I'm leaving you in charge."

Chip barked, her tail wagging in joy.

"Good girl." Detective Perez gave Laura one last nod and left, his gun at his side.

Laura locked the door behind him as instructed. "Let's get this placed cleaned up."

She pulled on her bright yellow gloves and picked up Chip's soiled puppy pads. In ordinary circumstances, Chip would get to go outside and run around after being locked up in the house. Not now. With Detective Perez scouring the grounds and a possible stalker hanging out there, Laura didn't trust Chip not to get hurt. So, she fed her some kibble and gave her some extra treats.

Chip ate the treats, but afterwards climbed onto her dog bed with a full on pout.

"I know, girl, and I'm sorry. This stalker isn't making it easy for either of us." Laura squatted down and patted her head.

Like most evenings of late, Laura slept sitting upright in her favorite chair. Chip lay curled up in her dog bed. The fire burned low, chasing the early morning spring chill away. From the pond, frogs sang their mating songs, and birds did the same high above in the neighboring trees.

Through the haze of light slumber, Laura heard it. She found comfort in nature's renewal and tried to burrow and relax fully into sleep's embrace.

It wouldn't come.

She was jolted awake by Chip barking her head off in alarm.

Her hand went to the gun beside her on the end table. Groggy, Laura got to her feet, just as Chip leapt off her dog bed and raced toward the door. Laura followed, her gun pointed, her stomach churning, and adrenaline narrowing her vision.

"Who's there?" Laura shouted. The words shook.

No response. Just the bang of something against the door.

"I'm armed!" Laura warned, raising the gun, and pointing it at the door. "I'm calling the police."

Laura backed away, realizing her phone remained on the end table. She'd grabbed her weapon but not the phone. She hissed at her foolishness.

In moments before Laura could react, the front door caved, and a black blur burst through the door's opening like a tornado. He plowed into her, tackling her hard to the floor. She crashed to the ground, sending her gun spiraling across the tile. Chip barked and growled before jumping into the fray and biting the assailant.

Disoriented, Laura reached out for something—anything—tangible. His breath's funk brushed her nose, sending her pinwheeling backwards, scrabbling to get away from both the smell and the violence. She struggled to make sense of her surroundings. Despite the early morning, most of her home remained in shadow. With her adrenaline pumping, everything looked different in shadow.

Damn it! He's in my house! Where's the gun?

He snatched Chip and threw her against the wall. She landed with a sickening *thud.*

Then he turned on Laura with homicidal rage.

"I told you I'd be seeing you." The hulking figure wore a ski mask, gloves, and all black clothing. He resembled death made real. The scream stuck in Laura's throat. Less than six feet away, he lunged for her and she scrambled to flee. He held up a knife.

Laura's eyes darted around the floor in search of the gun. She glanced back to him and the blade, a hunting knife about ten inches long. *Oh. Goddess.*

The white-hot pain in her shoulder forced her to stumble. She could feel the warmth pouring down her back.

"Fucking bitch!" he growled against her neck as another pain surged in her neck.

Laura jerked at the last minute, but the knife bit into the tender spot above her collar bone. She slammed her elbow into him with as much strength as she could muster.

I will not die today!

She smashed her bare foot onto his shoe and swung her elbow again into his torso. Her attacker grunted, stumbled, and snickered at her efforts.

"You got spunk for an old ass woman!" He lifted his arm to stab her again.

Laura pushed back into him, making his stabbing direction awkward as he had tried for her chest, but got her forearm as she raised it over her heart. She screamed as now three stab wounds sung in agony.

Slick with blood, Laura managed to free herself and hurry to put distance between them. They'd moved down the hallway and into the kitchen. She put the island between them.

I have to call 911. Get a weapon.

She reached for the butcher knife from the knife block, but her right arms refused to cooperate. He stood there, leering, and laughing at her.

"You aren't glad to see me."

"I, I don't *know* you." Laura panted. The pain had unfurled and spread across her body like a wildfire. She clenched her teeth from the pain. It sharped her perspective. "Just. Leave. Me. Alone."

He flexed his wrist and came for her again. A rushing boulder plowed through the kitchen, around the island in her direction. Instead of standing and letting him bowl into her, Laura dropped to the floor, a move he hadn't expected. Using her upper body, she rammed her shoulder into his lower legs, her good arm hooked behind one of his legs, and swept him to the ground. She raised two sons who had been avid wrestling fans.

He shouted in surprise and once he hit the tile, grunted in pain.

At that moment, Chip came sailing through the air and landed on the man's face, biting and growling. She attacked with the ferociousness of a German shepherd. Snarling and scratching, her dog didn't give the man a second to breathe. He struggled to fight her off, but now that he had been lowered to her level, Chip had a small advantage.

Laura fled back to the hallway. She discovered her gun and snatched it from the floor with her left hand. Pain seared across her body, thumping in aching rage. Her limbs weighed a million pounds and she struggled to lift the gun. She bled everywhere. In her left hand the weapon felt foreign, not nearly as an extension of her right hand.

A yelp broke through Laura's blurred musing and she backed herself against the wall.

The ragged breathing announced him before his presence appeared. He had the knife, but his mask had been ripped to tethers. Laura managed a smile. Her canine defender had mauled the attacker.

"That takes care of your fucking dog. And to think, I bought that mutt gifts." He snatched off what remained of the mask. "Now, it's your turn."

Dark blond hair lay plastered against his head. Dark brown eyes marred by scratches and bites burned in anger. He had a moustache and pierced ears. He might have been handsome before Chip taught him a lesson, but now those scars would last.

As a warning to others.

"Did you hurt my dog?" Laura winced. Her vision blurred and she blinked rapidly to stay focus.

"I killed that bitch." He took a step toward her.

He didn't see the gun by her side.

He only saw a battered old woman.

"Wrong answer." Laura lifted the weapon, but her fingers fumbled over the trigger.

As he closed the distance between them in a breath. Laura screamed as he struck her again in the chest. She managed to get her fingers to work. With her body screaming in pain, she fired.

Again.

The attacker grunted and slumped onto her. His weight crashed against her, pinning her against the wall and forcing her to crumple to her knees along with him. She didn't know if he was alive or dead, but she screamed as she pushed him off of her.

Call 911! Call 911!

She dropped the gun. With blood pouring out of her chest, Laura struggled to make her way to the living room. Her hand covered her stab wound, but blood continued to escape. Warmth splayed through her fingers.

Her eyes were heavy, her body molasses, and her brain whirling. With sheer determination, she reached her chair, and her cellphone. She propped herself against the chair, grabbed her throw, and tied it as best she could with one hand around her stab wound to slow the bleeding.

She dialed 911.

"911. What is the nature of your emergency?" the operator asked.

"I've been stabbed. Attacked. Shot intruder." Laura's chest was aflame with pain. Breathing became harder. She hurried and gave her address, not waiting for the operator's questions. She may not be alive.

"Ma'am. Stay on the line. The police and paramedics are on their way."

"Detective Perez. Please…" Laura heard her words slur. Clouds overtook her vision, and she fought to keep her eyes open.

She lost.

Three days later

Laura awoke to the subdued lights and bleach aroma of a hospital room. Her right arm muscles felt tight and burned. It had been wrapped in gauze from her palm down to her elbow. Tubs, wires, and gauze created a 3-D painting of suffering. Beside her, a figure moved from the shadows.

She screamed. The monitors went berserk. Laura flailed. "Let me out! Help!"

Detective Perez's somber tone penetrated her shrieks. "It's me. Detective Perez."

Perez.

Flashbacks to her attack shot through her. She couldn't breathe. Shocked. Stunned. Frozen by the violent memories ripping through her. Laura shook all over.

A warm hand clasped her shoulder. "You're in the hospital. You're safe."

His soothing tone oriented her, and she laid back against the pillows, her face was damp with cold sweat. As she did so, she winced. Then she remembered the stab wound to her back shoulder. The skin itched beneath the gauze. *Stitches.*

"Am I?" Laura licked her dried lips and closed her eyes.

"Are you what?"

"Safe?"

"Yeah, uh, your stalker is dead." Perez removed his hand. "So, yeah, you're safe."

I killed him. I took his life. "Dead? I only meant to get away…" The hot pinprick of tears made her voice thicken with emotion.

"Laura, this isn't your fault."

"Yeah it is! I shot him, more than once." Regret pressed against her and she sipped in a breath before dissolving into tears. She couldn't move her arms like she wanted, and all of the cords and monitors and the smells overwhelmed her.

She cried.

"Laura, the paramedics got there. He was transported to the ER. He survived."

"Survived?" Laura frowned.

"You did shoot him, twice, but no real damage. They released him and we arrested him. He committed suicide in jail."

Perez stood beside her bed. Laura hadn't realized how penned up her emotions had been since the stalker began his campaign. It poured out in heaping hiccups, deep breaths, and bitter tears. Time inched on as she released all of her angst and sorrow.

Once spent, she opened her eyes. Perez handed her tissue, and she blew her nose.

"Chip?" she croaked, her chin shaking. She almost couldn't form the words.

Perez's face didn't change. "We got her to a vet hospital. She'll survive, but she took some damage. Broken rib. Stab wound. She's lucky to be alive."

Laura burst into a new bout of tears. "Thank the goddess."

Perez said, "You rest. You've been through a lot. Your friends have been by, uh Hector and Maggie. They brought you flowers and cards."

"Did someone call my kids?" Laura wiped her eyes.

"I was able to get in touch with Samantha."

Laura nodded. "Detective, who was he?"

Perez stopped at the foot of her bed with his cowboy hat midway to his head. "You should rest, Laura."

"Who was he?" She repeated.

"His name was Arnold Spruce. He worked at the Tradesman Grocer in the meat department. We think that's where he saw you. He was a loner. The forensic team is going through his studio apartment. This is pretty open and shut case, but we want to ensure we have all the evidence."

"I'm gonna be arrested?" Laura frowned.

"No. You rest. Let me handle the criminal case. Okay?" Detective Perez's usual calm changed. The squeak of annoyance at the end caught Laura's attention. And his. "I'm sorry. I'm angry with myself for not being there that night or for not sending a car around to protect you."

"You couldn't have known…"

"Yeah, but I knew he was escalating. Should've done more." Perez rubbed his head before plopping his hat on. "I'll be in touch. You have my number."

As Perez exited, a gasp drew Laura's attention to the doorway.

Samantha stood just inside, holding the door with one hand, and her other hand over her mouth.

"Mom!"

"Sam." Laura didn't want her daughter to worry but seeing her brought her joy. "Oh, Sam!"

Her daughter rushed into the room, dropped her purse onto the floor and hugged Laura tight.

"Ow! Ow!" Laura didn't let go despite the pain.

Once they let go, Samantha wiped tears from her eyes and removed her jacket. "What happened? I get this call from the Taos police stating someone broke into your house…"

"Yeah. I'm all right." Laura patted Samantha's hand.

"And Chipotle?" Samantha squeezed. "Mom, you could've been killed. I talked to the doctor, and your injuries…"

"Are healing." Laura smiled. *Oh, how much she looks like Dominic.* "I'm stable. Right? I haven't spoken to the doctor yet. How in the world did you?"

"I've been here for a few hours, mom," Samantha whispered. "You lost a lot of blood, and the knife nicked one of your lungs."

Laura grew quiet. She didn't know the extent of her injuries, but she did know it wasn't good as evident by the number of monitors. She had her own room, which meant they didn't think she was leaving any time soon. It didn't take a rocket scientist.

Nevertheless, Samantha's words took the wind out of her.

"Mom, what happened? Are you up to talking about it?" Samantha leaned in. "One cop said it was a home invasion. Way out where you live?"

Laura met her daughter's questioning gaze, saw it brimming with fear and love, and decided to keep her horror to herself.

"Bunny, they're dangerous people in the world. They do evil things for reasons we won't be able to understand. The only thing that matters is I'm safe. Chip is safe, and the stalker is dead."

"Wait. What? Stalker." Samantha stepped back. "Mom! You didn't tell me or Abe or anyone?"

Laura cursed her medicated tongue. "I didn't want to worry you or your brothers. I handled it."

"We love you, mom. You could've died, you stubborn old goat." Samantha hugged her, her face wet with tears. "Don't do that again."

Laura held her youngest. "I love you."

"I love you, too." Samantha pulled back. "Now, tell me everything and don't leave a thing out."

And she did.

The End

MEET BOBBY NASH

Although he doesn't run around getting into a lot of adventures like Abraham Snow, Bobby Nash spends his days writing about heroes who do. Bobby also never solved a murder he didn't commit (only in the literary sense, I assure you), he is an award-winning author of novels, comic books, short stories, novellas, graphic novels, and the occasional screenplay for a number of publishers and production companies.

In 2020, Bobby won Best Novel in the Pulp Factory Awards for Nightveil: Crisis at the Crossroads of Infinity and was awarded the Sangria Summit Society's New Pulp Fiction Award for his work on the SNOW series.

Bobby is a member of the International Association of Media Tie-in Writers and International Thriller Writers. For more information on Bobby Nash and his work, please visit him at www.bobbynash.com

MEET GARY PHILLIPS

Gary Phillips has written novels, novellas, over sixty-five short stories, comics and conceived what became the well-received Black Pulp I & II for Pro Se Productions. He's also written new pulp adventures for Moonstone Books, including the linked anthology Day of the Destroyers and Airship 27. The South Florida Sun-Sentinel said of his latest novel in a review, "With its echoes of the Doc Savage series and the Indiana Jones movies, Matthew Henson and the Ice Temple of Harlem should make for [a] long-running series."

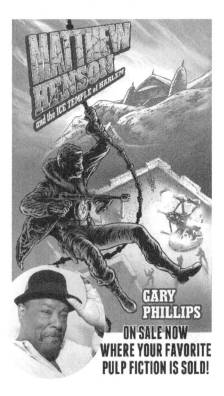

MEET NICOLE GIVENS KURTZ

Nicole Givens Kurtz is an author, editor, and educator. She's been named as one of Book Riot's Best Black Indie SFF Writers. She's also the editor of the groundbreaking anthology, SLAY: Stories of the Vampire Noire. Her novels have been a finalist in the Dream Realm Awards, Fresh Voices, and EPPIE Awards for science fiction. She's written for White Wolf, Bram Stoker Finalist in Horror Anthology, Sycorax's Daughters, and Serial Box's The Vela: Salvation series. Nicole has over 40 short stories published as well as 11 novels and three active speculative mystery series. She's a member of Horror Writers Association, Sisters in Crime, and Science Fiction Writers of America. You can support her work via Patreon.

MEET JEFFREY HAYES

JEFFREY RAY HAYES is a freelance illustrator and graphic designer living in the Austin area of Central Texas. He began his career doing pen and ink art and magazine layout work for Austin-based table-top gaming companies. Jeff also spent time working as a commercial artist and display designer for a Texas-based grocery company in the 1980s until he made a career change. He has served for 30 years as a police officer until his retirement in 2019 as an assistant police chief. During that time, he never stopped working as a freelance artist and formed Plasmafire Graphics, LLC.

Jeff has worked on a number of television / web-based productions and independent films in the United States and United Kingdom as a graphic artist, creating promotional materials and key art for entertainment industry marketing. His work has also extended to book cover illustration, where he has completed over 200 pieces that have graced the covers of books and magazines.

Being only self-taught in illustration and graphic design, he is currently attending the Gemini School of Visual Arts to attain that long-overdue Visual Arts and Communications Degree. The degree will consume much of his time from 2020-2024, but he looks forward to taking on freelance work again when the course of training is done.

Visit Jeffrey Hayes at www.plasmafiregraphics.com/

MEET STUART GAUFFI

Stuart first began exercising his fascination with vocal performance at a very young age, steeped in performances of the golden age of Mel Blanc, June Foray and dozens of other virtuosos of the radio, early television, film, and cartoon worlds. The result was much parental head-shaking, with an ever-increasing number of odd sounds emanating from those young vocal cords. What's followed has been a life of performance on stage, radio, industrial film, and various digital media including dozens of audiobooks.

If you like listening to a good story (or even just the occasional ripping good yarn), Stuart would love to tell you one.

Learn more about Stuart Gauffi aka <u>That Famous Guy</u> at www.thatfamousguy.com.

SPECIAL THANKS!

A big tip of the snow cap to Nicole Givens Kurtz and Gary Phillips for joining #TeamSnow and bringing new tales of Mama Snow and Big John Salmon to life. As always, I'm thrilled to have the art of Jeffrey Hayes grace Snow's covers. Also, big thanks to Stuart Gauffi for making the Snow audio books come alive. I have a great team. They're the best.

A HUGE THANK YOU to my Patrons for supporting my work on Patreon. I appreciate each and every one of you and I hope you enjoyed getting a copy of SNOW STAR a few days before everyone else. There are perks to being a Patron and you are the greatest. Thanks to James Burns, Robert McIntyre, Lil' John Nacinovich, Sean R. Reid, John Kilgallon, Andrea Judy, Darrell Grizzle, Jack D. Kammerer Jr., Jeff Allen, Caine Dorr, Colin Joss, Adam Messer, David Perlmutter, Brian K. Morris, Jeffrey Hayes, and Michael Stackpole. Rock stars one and all. Your support is appreciated.

NOW ON SALE

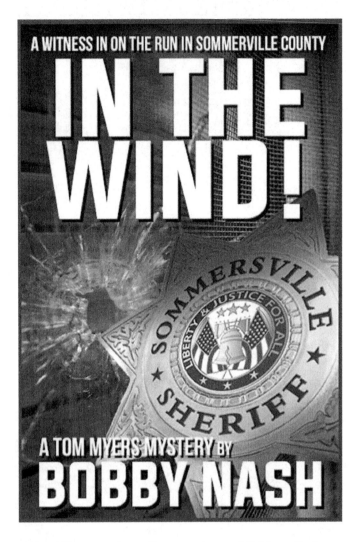

Sheriff Tom Myers Returns in an All-New Series.

When the look of your book matters to you.
And it should, because it matters to your potential readers.

Cover Illustration • Marketing Artwork • Social Media Graphics • Posters
Title Design • Book Jacket Layout • Promotional Videos • Logos / Branding

Professional illustrations at indie author pricing.

PLASMAFIREGRAPHICS
PLASMAFIREGRAPHICS.COM
PLASMAFIREGRAPHICS ON
JEFFREY.HAYES@PLASMAFIREGRAPHICS.COM

COMING SOON

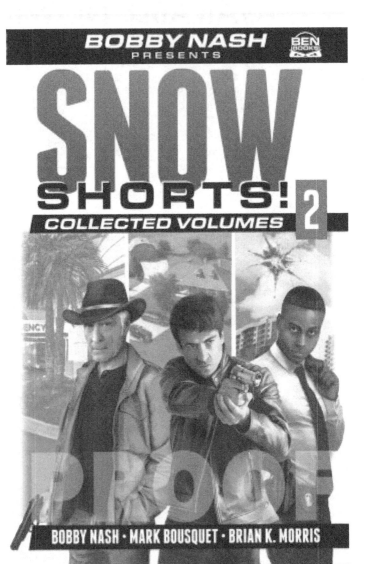

COMING SOON

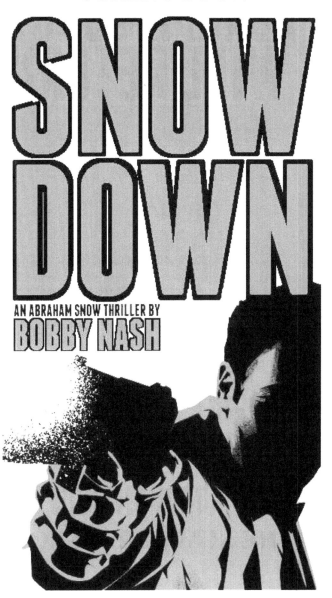

ABRAHAM SNOW WILL RETURN

WWW.ABRAHAMSNOW.COM
#THE SUMMEROFSNOW

69245247R00096